## CHAPTER ONE

He'd been conned.

Ronin Cooper stepped out of the warehouse and shook his head. Somehow, Darcy Ward had tricked him into doing a coffee run for the entire Treasure Hunter Security team. He jogged down the front steps of the building that housed the THS offices. As a former Navy SEAL and CIA agent, he should have seen it coming. Still, Darcy could get pretty mean and sneaky when it came to her caffeine.

As he headed down the sidewalk, he pulled in a deep breath of air. Spring had hit Denver with a vengeance, and all around, the trees were bursting with green leaves and any lingering chill of winter had left the air. The renovated warehouse that housed THS was on the edge of LoDo, not far from Coors Field, home of the Colorado Rockies. Ronin wasn't a huge baseball fan, but when he wasn't off guarding some archeological dig or museum exhibition, he and the gang sometimes caught a game.

As he turned a corner, the city of Denver rose up ahead of him. Overhead, the sun shone, as it always did here. It was nice to be in the light, and most days, he realized he was getting used to it.

No more blood-soaked battlefields or dark back-alley activities. His muscles tensed, one by one, and Ronin stuck his hands in the pockets of his cargo pants. He'd spent so long working in the dark—on his SEAL missions, for the CIA. Hell, he'd been born in the dark.

He set his shoulders back and pushed those thoughts away. He'd gotten out—maybe not without losing a few chunks of his soul—but he worked for THS now. He worked with people he liked, and most of the time he enjoyed the job. He even liked Denver. He could cycle in the summer, and snowboard in the winter. Many a weekend, he went climbing with Callum Ward, one of the owners of THS. After walking in the shadows for so long, he was coming to realize that he liked his life just the way it was.

As he approached the baseball park, traffic got a little busier. Suddenly, the hair on the back of his neck stood up and every one of his instincts told him he was being followed. The government had spent a hell of a lot of money ensuring Ronin's instincts were finely-honed.

He kept his stride and body relaxed. He didn't want to alert his pursuer.

He wondered who the hell it was. THS had royally pissed off Silk Road on their last mission in Africa. They'd even finally managed to take down one of the top people in the dangerous, black-market antiquities group.

His boss, Declan Ward, had warned them all that Silk Road would be out for payback, and to stay sharp.

Ronin paused at some stop lights, waiting to cross the street. He casually turned his head and scanned his surroundings. He spotted a flash of color. Hair that was a deep copper hue that made him think of the rising sun.

It was *her*.

He'd spied her three times before. Once, at Dec and Layne's wedding. Mystery Woman had gatecrashed the reception and had been watching the THS gang. When Ronin had spotted her, she'd taken off. Another time, he'd seen her watching him cycling on one of the bike paths he used a lot. The third time, he'd seen her at the bar where he and his friends sometimes grabbed a beer after work. Once again, she'd disappeared before he'd reached her.

Who the hell was she?

Ronin strode across the street. Now, he was in the heart of LoDo, with its brick buildings and renovated warehouses. Ahead, he spotted the narrow entrance to an alley and turned into it. Brick walls rose up on either side. There were a handful of doorways and puddles on the ground, but other than that, the alley was empty.

He walked deeper into the shadows that he knew so well. Then, he quickly moved into a doorway, crouching so he was hidden by darkness.

Moments later, he heard footsteps—light and quick. Definitely a woman. Then he heard a feminine curse and he raised a brow. That wasn't very ladylike.

He let out a slow breath, his heartbeat calm and

controlled. He charged out of his hiding place and grabbed the woman.

He saw wide blue eyes, and blunt, copper-colored bangs above them.

As he tightened his hold on her, she cursed like a sailor again. Before he could speak, she landed a sharp kick to his knee.

Surprised, he stumbled. Hell, *no one* surprised him.

By the time he'd righted himself, the woman was running out of the alley.

*Oh, no, you don't.* Ronin broke into a sprint.

She was fast, and he guessed there was a fit body under her jeans and shirt. Seconds later, he wrapped his arms around her from behind and lifted her off her feet.

She started kicking and struggling. "Help! Someone help me."

"Stop. I'm not going to hurt you," he growled.

"Let me go!"

"Not until we talk."

"Help! Fire!"

Her struggles increased. Damn, she was strong, too.

"Fire! Fire!" she yelled.

Fire? She'd obviously heard the old adage about people being more likely to help if there was fire, but not an unknown threat. He spun her, pushed her into a doorway and backed her up against the wall.

She lifted her chin. She was a little over five-foot, but acted like she was six feet tall. Her blue eyes flashed. Again, she opened her mouth to scream—

"Stop it," he said. "Tell me who you are."

*SHIT*. She'd seriously underestimated him.

Peri Butler looked up into the dark, lean face. It was a little too sharp and dangerous to be considered anything as civilized as handsome. But there was something about him that made you want to look at him. And keep looking at him.

There was sexy stubble on his strong jaw, and eyes that she'd thought were black or brown, but were actually a very dark blue. He watched her with a steady, intense gaze that left her feeling stripped bare.

This was a man who would dig and dig until he knew every one of your secrets.

*Shit. Shit.* Peri repeated her favorite curse word a few more times in her head. From her research on Treasure Hunter Security, she knew his name was Ronin Cooper. But she didn't know him, and she certainly couldn't trust him.

She dropped her weight, and, once again, she realized she'd surprised him. He staggered to catch her, but she twisted, pressed a palm to the dirty ground—*yuck*, she so wasn't going to think about that right now—and managed to jerk away. With a spin, she broke out from between his hard body and the wall.

But she'd barely taken one step when he grabbed the back of her shirt and yanked backward. Arms wrapped around her, feeling like hard bands of steel. She was yanked back against a hard, muscled body that radiated heat.

"Name. Now." His deep voice was a rumble against her left ear.

"Screw you."

"Why have you been spying on me and Treasure Hunter Security?"

He'd seen her? *Damn*. She knew he'd spotted her at the wedding, but not the other times.

"Do you work for Silk Road?" he demanded.

That name made her stiffen. "No!"

His voice lowered. "If I find out you do..."

His tone raised goosebumps on Peri's skin. He didn't need to finish the threat. She believed he was a dangerous man capable of anything.

She worried her lip. It didn't sound like he liked Silk Road much. So, he and THS probably weren't a part of that horrible organization... God, she was so confused, and didn't know who to trust.

She couldn't risk her twin sister's life.

The thought that Amber was hurt—or, God forbid, dead—filled Peri with despair. She *had* to find her sister, and she'd do whatever she had to.

"Tell me your name," Ronin Cooper said again.

Could she trust him? After watching him and the others he worked with, she was pretty sure they were the real deal. But Amber's life hung in the balance...

"All right, fine. We'll do this the hard way," he ground out.

Just as Peri stiffened, the world spun, and she was lifted off her feet. He tossed her over a hard shoulder.

For a second, she was speechless, dangling upside down.

"Hey!" She banged a hand against his back. Beneath his shirt, he was as hard as a rock.

"I gave you a chance to talk." He strode out of the alley. "You didn't take it."

Back on the sidewalk, he headed back toward the THS offices. Peri let out a stream of curses, some in a few different languages.

"You talk to your mother with that mouth?" Ronin drawled.

Peri lifted her head and looked around. Surely someone would help her. "My mother taught me some of those."

As her captor stomped down the path, people eyed him curiously, but no one intervened.

"I'll talk," she said. "Just put me down."

"You'll talk." His tone was dark.

Peri screwed up her nose. "Are you always this bossy and unforgiving?"

"Yes."

She huffed out a breath. "You're not very nice."

"I don't care."

Peri grumbled under her breath and looked down. She had to admit she had a very good view of a deliciously firm ass encased in dark-gray cargo pants.

*Jeez, Peri. Don't look at his ass.*

She twisted and saw the warehouse just ahead. She knew it had once been an old flour mill, until siblings Declan, Callum, and Darcy Ward had purchased it. They'd renovated it and started their security business together. Peri had researched all she could about them. They appeared to be legit, and their business well run.

But they were often linked with Silk Road in the press, and she wasn't sure if Treasure Hunter Security was just another front for the dark, shadowy, black-market ring.

Her gut cramped. She knew she needed help to find Amber. A part of her prayed that Mr. Dark-and-Unfriendly, and the others at THS, could help her... because she was running out of options.

Peri squeezed her eyes closed. Amber was running out of time.

## CHAPTER TWO

R onin strode up the steps and used his shoulder to push open the glass doors into the warehouse.

His boots echoed on the polished concrete floor. He passed the stairs that led up to Dec and Layne's apartment above the office and headed toward the lounge area. The huge, open-plan space had large windows that offered a fantastic view of downtown Denver. The brick wall at the far end of the warehouse was covered in computer screens. Sleek desks in that same corner held high-end computers. That was Darcy's domain.

There was a small kitchenette tucked into another corner, and a huge conference table dominated the middle of the space. Off to one side was his destination, where couches were grouped together by a pool table and an air hockey table.

Darcy looked up from her computer. One of her silky brows rose, and she tucked a strand of her chin-length dark hair behind her ear. "That's not my latte, Coop."

"Nope." He stomped past the conference table, toward the battered couches. Darcy kept threatening to replace them, but Ronin guessed she hadn't done it yet because she was worried they'd wreck the new ones.

Logan O'Connor's big form was currently sprawled in an armchair. He raised his head, his shaggy hair falling over his face. "What have you got there, Coop?"

"A spy." Ronin set the woman on her feet.

Hearing footsteps, Ronin glanced over and saw Declan approach. In well-worn jeans and a black T-shirt, he looked every inch the former SEAL he was.

The woman straightened, gripping the hem of her white shirt and tugging it down. She scanned the room, taking it all in. He could tell she was nervous by the tense way she held herself, but there was no fear on her face. She lifted her chin.

She was a pretty thing, in a unique kind of way. Her hair color was one of a kind. She had the copper strands pulled back in a ponytail, and her bangs were cut bluntly across her eyes. And those big, blue eyes...they could swallow a man whole.

Ronin had always liked unique. He was good at seeing beneath the obvious.

"I'm not a spy," the woman said.

"Talk." Ronin crossed his arms over his chest. "I want your name, and I want to know why you've been watching us."

"*This* is the person you said has been watching us?" Dec said, curiosity on his face.

Darcy wandered closer, with the elegant Sydney by

her side. Logan's girlfriend ran the business side of THS. They both eyed the woman curiously.

His captive drew herself up. "My name is Peri Butler. I've been watching you to see if I could trust you."

Ronin raised a brow. He'd been trained to read body language, and right now she was using stubborn confidence to hide desperation and fear. Unless she was a really, really good liar, she was telling the truth. "Strange way to go about it."

Peri wrapped her arms around her middle. "I needed to make sure you didn't work for Silk Road."

From nearby, Logan made a choking sound. "Fucking hate Silk Road."

Dec was watching her steadily. "Go on."

"I know you've tangled with them, but I wasn't sure if it was just a front. Silk Road is good at lies and subterfuge."

"They are," Ronin agreed. She looked his way, and this time, he saw sadness and worry in her blue eyes. "I can assure you, we're on the opposite side to Silk Road. What's your link to them?"

She hesitated.

That's when Darcy strode over with a click of heels. She held out a hand to the woman. "If we can help you, we will."

Peri looked back at Ronin. "Six weeks ago, I was approached to guide an expedition. My sister and I are both experienced guides. It looked legit, and they were offering a lot of money. A lot." She shook her head. "But something was off. The guy who approached me, a good-looking Australian, gave me the heebie-jeebies."

"Heebie-jeebies?" Ronin said slowly.

She waved a hand. "I know tough guys like you don't use terms like that, but the guy was off."

Ronin understood instincts and he knew when someone was off.

"He gave me a company name. Karakorum, Inc. The company had a website, and it looked professional, but I still didn't like it."

Darcy cleared her throat. "The southern route of the historical Silk Road ran through the Karakorum Mountains on the border of Pakistan and China. It was called the Karakorum route."

Something flickered over Peri's face. "Shit. I should have dug deeper. I turned the job down, but my sister, Amber...she was between jobs, bored, and looking for something to do. She's an adventurer at heart. We were raised traveling all over the world." Peri pressed her lips together. "My parents are free-spirits, and said the world was our school." She dragged in a deep breath. "I own a climbing gym, Anti-Gravity, down near the University of Denver. I take guide jobs occasionally, but the gym's busy right now."

"Hey, I've heard good things about that gym," Logan said. "Think Cal's been there before."

"Her story checks out." Darcy looked up from her tablet. "Except it appears your legal name is Peridot Butler."

Peri winced. "Yes, thanks to my mother, my sister and I ended up named after gems. But I don't answer to Peridot. It's Peri."

"Your sister took the job?" Ronin said, pushing the conversation back on track.

"Yes." Peri's eyes closed. "She went, and I've lost contact with her." Her eyes opened again, and Ronin couldn't look away. "She was supposed to have been back a week ago. The website for the company's gone, and all the phone numbers are disconnected. I did some digging, and found out that the website had originally been listed to a shell company that linked back to Silk Road."

Ronin shared a look with Dec. This wasn't sounding good. "Where was the expedition headed?"

Peri swallowed. "My sister and I are experienced polar guides. We specialize in ice expeditions, and glacier and crevasse travel." She twisted her hands together. "The expedition went to Antarctica."

---

PERI SAT at the long conference table, staring at the polished wood surface. Someone set a hot mug of coffee down in front of her.

She looked up at Ronin. "Thanks."

The rest of the THS team sat around the table, and as Peri sipped the coffee, she wondered if Amber was warm, and had food and drink. If she was still alive.

"I wouldn't be very thankful, because Dec made the coffee today." Darcy Ward sat in the chair beside Peri. "That's why I sent Coop out to the coffee shop."

A blonde woman in a fitted skirt and classy blouse sat on the other side of the table. Peri knew from her research that she was Sydney Granger, former CEO of Granger

Industries. Both Sydney and Darcy were polished and elegant, and made Peri feel rumpled and disheveled.

"We'd like to help you," Darcy said.

Sydney leaned forward. "THS helped me find my brother. Silk Road had kidnapped him in South America."

Peri had read the articles about the fantastic adventure into the Peruvian cloud forests. Sydney's brother had been rescued by THS, alive. Peri had so badly wanted to believe the story was true.

"I can pay your going rate," Peri said. While her gym was still growing, she had a good nest egg. "Polar guiding pays very well." And Peri wasn't the kind of woman to spend a fortune on clothes and jewelry. No, she spent her money mainly on climbing gear, and on the house she'd recently purchased.

The big man with the shaggy hair, Logan O'Connor, came up behind Sydney, resting his hands on the woman's slim shoulders. Peri had read that these two were a couple. At first glance, they looked like complete opposites, but even after knowing them for just a few minutes, she could see that they fit. Sydney was always smiling at Logan, and the man watched Sydney with a heated, possessive warmth in his eyes.

Peri had never had a man who'd looked at her that way. She'd dated a long string of adrenaline junkies who were always looking for a good time, and that was about it. She had a weakness for hard, muscled male bodies.

"So, the expedition left a month ago?" Ronin's voice cut through her thoughts.

Peri cleared her throat. "Just over. It was a four-week

trip to take ice samples and monitor the rising temperatures on the Antarctic ice sheet."

"Silk Road are black market antiquities thieves," Ronin said. "They're not interested in ice samples or global warming."

"I know that. That had to be their cover story. But I know there are no antiquities or ruins in Antarctica, so I'm at a loss to know what they were after."

"Could they be after relics from early Antarctic explorers?" Sydney asked.

Dec drummed his fingers against the table. "A few years back, old huts used by the early explorers were uncovered. They were perfectly preserved. They were like time capsules, filled with lots of old items. Tinned food, bottles of whiskey, journals written by the explorers."

"But nothing valuable enough for Silk Road to find it interesting," Ronin said.

"Right," Dec agreed. "Peri, do you have any information on where this expedition was headed exactly?"

Peri shook her head, pushing back the all-too-familiar despair. "I don't know. Somewhere near the Ellsworth Mountains." She blew out a breath. "I realized something was wrong a couple of days before they were due back."

Ronin frowned. "Before?"

She nodded. "Amber left a strange voicemail on my phone." Peri pulled her phone out of her pocket. She set it on the table and hit the speaker button. The message played.

"Find it, Peri. 1881, 17$^{th}$, 12, 22, 112, 1971."

"She must have gotten access to a satellite phone," Dec mused.

"What do the numbers mean?" Ronin asked.

"I don't know." Peri lifted her shoulder, battling back the frustration chewing at her belly. "I've tried to decipher it, but it doesn't mean anything to me."

Darcy pulled out a sleek tablet and started tapping on the screen. "I'll run some searches and see if anything pops. I'll also start searching to see what might have sparked Silk Road's interest in Antarctica."

Sydney stood. "I'll make a few calls and see if I can track supplies or flights for an expedition to the Ellsworth Mountains."

Dec nodded. "I'll make a few calls, too."

"Thank you." A moment later, Peri found herself sitting at the table with only Ronin for company. "Sorry for spying on you."

"It's fine. You weren't that good at it."

She snorted. "You didn't catch me the first few times. And I got away from you twice. I almost got away from you this last time, too."

"Almost doesn't count."

Peri gripped her hands together. "Amber is a great guide and good in the snow."

"Then it sounds like she has all the skills she needs to survive this," Ronin said.

"By the time we were twelve, we'd both visited Antarctica before. Not to mention, climbed the Himalayas, trekked through the Sahara, and dived with sharks in Australia."

"Sounds exciting."

"It was, but...sometimes you just want to stay in one place for a while. To not live out of the bag."

"I wouldn't really know."

She looked into his lean face. "I just bought a house. And I'm going to get a dog." Everything inside her went cold. "My sister is my family. I love our parents, but they're currently living in an ashram in India. I don't think they'll ever stop traveling. But Amber wanted to be here in Denver with me, as well."

A big hand covered hers. "We'll find her."

His skin was so warm, and his touch surprisingly comforting. She gripped his fingers. "You can't promise that, but thank you."

Suddenly, there was a muted *ping* from the computers nearby.

Darcy scooted her office chair over and tapped a screen. Her beautiful face froze. "Holy cow." She was scanning whatever was on the screen. "Everyone needs to see this." She leaped up and her fingers flew over a keyboard. An image filled one of the screens on the wall.

Peri's chest tightened, filling with anticipation, worry, excitement. Was this good news or bad? She stood, and, keeping hold of Ronin's hand, they moved closer to the screens.

Everyone gathered, studying the aerial image of an ice plain.

Peri frowned. She guessed it was somewhere in Antarctica. A few darker, rocky, mountain peaks poked through the ice.

"Antarctica. So?" Declan said.

Darcy tapped the screen and the image zoomed in.

"This shot is from the western side of the continent. The ice is melting faster on that side, and it's uncovering mountains that haven't been free of ice and snow in years. There's been some recent chatter on the internet..."

The image zoomed in again. Everyone gasped.

Peri blinked. Surely that wasn't what she thought it was.

She looked up and saw Ronin's jaw was tight. He didn't have the most expressive face, but she got the sense that he was as equally shocked as she was.

"Is that a *pyramid*?" Ronin said.

## CHAPTER THREE

R onin stared at the screen.

There *couldn't* be a pyramid rising out of the snow in Antarctica. He studied the symmetrical sides of the structure.

"It could be natural," Dec said.

Ronin shook his head. That thing didn't look natural to him.

"Hey, where is everyone?" a voice called out.

Dr. Layne Ward strode in, a bag on her shoulder. Dec moved over to claim a kiss from his wife. "Hey there, Dr. Ward. You might be able to help us out here."

"Oh? Nice to be needed." Layne's gaze settled on Peri. "Hi. I'm Layne Ward." She shot a smile at Dec. "Saying that never gets old."

Dec hugged his new wife harder.

"Layne, this is Peri Butler," Ronin said. "Her sister joined an expedition as a guide and hasn't returned."

Layne's face turned serious. "I'm sorry to hear that, Peri."

"Turns out the expedition was funded by Silk Road," Dec added.

The archeologist dumped her bag on the conference table. "Now I'm really sorry to hear that." She looked at her husband. "Are we going to help out?"

"Yes," Ronin replied. He sensed Peri looking at him, but turned back to the screen.

"The expedition was to Antarctica. Peri and her sister Amber are polar guides."

"Antarctica?" Layne frowned. "Silk Road goes after invaluable ancient antiquities. There was no civilization in Antarctica."

Ronin saw Peri's shoulders slump.

"You're sure?" Peri asked.

"The continent's been covered by ice for millions of years," Layne said, sympathy on her face.

"So, what's that?" Peri pointed at the screen.

Layne looked up at the image and blinked. She moved forward, her brow creasing. "I have no idea."

"Think it could be manmade?" Dec asked.

"Oh, my God." Layne was quiet for a moment. "It certainly looks too regular to be natural and has similar proportions to many Egyptian pyramids."

The room fell silent, and Ronin noticed the way that Dec was watching his wife.

"You know something else?" Dec prompted.

Layne ran a hand through her brown hair. "Well, now that I think about it, I remember seeing some documents we combed through for a previous mission. The Ahnenerbe was interested in Antarctica."

"Shit." Dec thrust his hands on his hips. "This is shades of Madagascar again, isn't it?"

Peri's brows pulled together. "Ahnenerbe?"

"Hitler's archeological group, tasked with proving the Aryan race was real." Layne's nose wrinkled. "It seemed they also believed that there were advanced civilizations that existed on Earth thousands of years ago. Civilizations that left possible advanced technology behind."

Peri blinked. "Like aliens?"

"No." Layne smiled and shook her head. "There is some evidence that, while not proven, could show that advanced human cultures existed that pre-date current beliefs. One of our other THS members, Morgan, has a boyfriend who is a bit of an expert in this. He's been trying to convince me that advanced cultures existed, and may have been destroyed at the end of the last ice age."

"So, what did the Nazis think was in Antarctica?" Ronin asked.

Layne shook her head. "I don't know. There wasn't a lot of detail in the reports I read."

Darcy tapped one of her nails against her lips. "I'll see what I can find."

Dec nodded. "Layne, call Morgan and Zach. I know they have a few days off, but see if they can come in. And Darcy, I want you to talk to..."

"Special Agent Arrogant and Annoying." Darcy grimaced.

Dec ran his tongue over his teeth. "Yes."

Darcy heaved out a beleaguered sigh. "I'll make the call."

There was another *ping* from Darcy's computer. She hurried over, tapping on the screen.

"Something's come back on the search running for the words and numbers in your sister's message." Darcy looked up, meeting Peri's gaze. "God, 1881 was the year Union Station opened on 17th and Wynkoop streets."

Peri leaped to her feet, hope on her face. "That's both 1881 and 17th. What about the other numbers?"

"12, 22, and 112. Union Station has twelve train tracks, twenty-two gates in the bus station, and one-hundred-and-twelve rooms in the hotel in the historical terminal building."

"And 1971?" Ronin asked.

Darcy shook her head. "No luck on that one. I can't match it to anything, yet."

Ronin gripped Peri's shoulders. "Your sister must have left you something at Union Station."

"How could she get something there from Antarctica?"

"She might have sent it on her way down to Antarctica? They would have stopped in South America to get supplies."

Peri nodded. "If she'd realized something was off, she might have sent me something, just in case. Then called and left me the message when things went bad. But why not send it to me directly?"

"Because she was afraid Silk Road was watching you," he said.

She shivered. "I should never have let her go."

"Who would she send something to? Does she know someone who works at Union Station?"

"I don't know all her friends. She likes to go out and party. She has loads of friends."

"Think, Peri."

"I am." She shoved her hand through her hair.

"They might work at the hotel," Ronin suggested.

"And there are several restaurants and shops," Darcy said. "Let me see if...found something!" She looked up, her blue-gray eyes gleaming. "There's a Tattered Cover bookstore in the terminal, and the first store opened in 1971."

"Amber and I go to the Tattered Cover a lot! The one on Colfax." Peri sucked in a breath. "She has a friend who works there and floats between stores, I think. Stella, no, Sam...Stacey!"

Darcy snatched up the phone on her desk, tapped in a number, and pressed it to her ear. "Hello, is this the Tattered Cover Union Station? Is Stacey working today? She is? Great, thank you." Darcy ended the call.

"I need to get there," Peri said.

Ronin looked at Dec. "I'll take her."

Dec nodded. "We'll keep working at this end. Be careful."

Ronin was always careful. He led Peri outside. She was vibrating with energy as he led her over to his bike.

"Where's your car?"

"Parked in the garage of my condo." He nodded at his bike. "This is my ride."

"We're riding on that?"

He handed her his extra helmet. "It's not far."

She took the helmet and smiled. "I've ridden a few motorcycles, but they were rickety, noisy things for riding through rice paddies or down jungle tracks."

He swung onto the bike. "Well, you're in for a treat." He gestured for her to climb on behind him. "I'll take care of you, Peri."

"Are you trustworthy, Ronin?"

"No."

She eyed him for a second before she pulled the helmet on, leaving the visor up. She settled behind him. "Is there a handle for me to hold on to?"

"You hold on to me."

She gingerly wrapped her arms around his waist. Ronin gunned the engine and pulled out. Peri quickly leaned forward, her arms gripping onto him, hard.

He set off down the street, weaving through the traffic. She was a pleasant weight behind him. He'd never had a woman on his bike. Hell, he generally avoided women.

Union Station wasn't far away. He pulled in to park at the front of the historic main building, and ignored a quick, niggling feeling of disappointment that the ride was already over. He glanced up at the bright-orange letters that spelled out Union Station above the entrance.

He turned back, and helped Peri unfasten the helmet. She looked up at him with flushed cheeks, her eyes glittering with pleasure.

"After this is all over, will you take me for a ride again some time?" she asked, her voice husky.

*Shit.* Ronin's cock instantly went hard. She was

looking at him just how he imagined she'd look if he'd spent time touching her, stroking her, kissing her.

But then he remembered what she'd said to him back at the office. She was looking to settle down and make a home. Ronin wasn't the home-and-hearth kind of guy, and never would be.

He climbed off the bike. "Come on, let's find this bookstore."

They walked into the station's Great Hall. Ronin waited a second for his eyes to adjust to stepping out of the bright sunlight. The building had been renovated some time ago, and the Great Hall was the main waiting area, rimmed by bars, the hotel, and shops. It was decorated in a grand, historic style, with lots of bright white, and accents in black and gold. Several people were striding through the space, dragging suitcases or carrying bags, heading for the modern train hall and bus station behind the main building. He spotted the bookstore and pointed it out.

Peri swiveled. She looked like a woman on a mission. He could easily picture her leading an expedition. He looked around. No one appeared to be watching them, or paying them any interest. *Good.*

They stepped inside the shop. The small space was packed with shelves that were loaded with books. A bookcase near the front displayed a number of train-themed books.

Skirting the shelves, Peri scanned the staff member at the desk. A young man. She shook her head. "I don't see Stacey. I think she's blonde."

"There." He spotted a young woman standing on a stool, organizing some shelves at the back of the store.

Peri approached the woman. "Stacey?"

The woman spun and gasped, the multitude of bracelets on her wrist tinkling. "Amber!"

"No, I'm her sister, Peri."

Stacey stepped off the stool, giving Ronin a wary look before focusing on Peri again. "Right. You guys look similar, but aren't identical."

"Did she—?"

"Yes. I have no idea why she sent me something to the shop. It was postmarked from somewhere called Punta Arenas. She wrote that I had to take the package to an address in the mountains and put it in a secret hiding place. All very cloak and dagger." Stacey smiled like it was all good fun. "Her note said to tell no one but you, if you came in."

Peri's face fell. "The mountains?"

The woman should never play poker. Ronin could read every emotion on her face. He mentally shook his head. He'd spent a lifetime being trained to not show his emotion.

Stacey nodded. "She said you'd know where."

"I do," Peri said. "Thanks. Did you see what was in there?"

Stacey shook her head. "Sorry. It was small and the envelope was sealed."

"Thanks again, Stacey."

"Hey, when is Amber back from her trip?" the blonde asked, confusion on her face. She was clearly picking up that something was wrong.

Ronin watched Peri's lip tremble before she firmed it and forced a smile. "Soon."

As they left the shop, Ronin found himself sliding an arm across her shoulders.

She looked up at him. "Are we acting as a couple?" she whispered.

"I thought you looked...upset."

"Are you giving me a hug?"

"I...don't really hug." Time to change the subject. "You know where this package from your sister is?"

Peri nodded. "My gram, my mother's mother, had a cabin up in the mountains. It's about two hours out of Denver. Amber and I spent lots of vacations there with Gram. She left it to us when she passed away." Peri squeezed her eyes closed for a second. "God, what did Amber get herself into? All this secrecy. What if she's dead?" Pain vibrated through her voice.

Ronin touched a finger to her chin and lifted it until she met his gaze. "You don't know that. Don't make up nightmares, just focus on the facts." He reached for her hand. "Let's get back to the office, I'll grab my truck, and we'll head up into the mountains."

She sniffed. "Thanks. Now I think I really do need a hug."

"I'm not the hugging type." Although, Ronin was surprised by the unfamiliar urge to want to make her feel better. He wanted to see that terrible tension on her face melt away.

"Everyone likes hugs, Ronin. You obviously just haven't had enough practice." She leaned forward and wrapped her arms around him.

Ronin stood there, looking down at her copper hair. Then he lifted one hand and pressed it to her slim back. She gripped him tighter, and he ran his hand up and down her spine.

Finally, she pulled back and looked at him, a small smile on her face. "See, there you go. That didn't hurt, did it?"

"No."

Her smile faded and her gaze dropped to his lips.

*Damn.* The last thing Ronin needed was an insane attraction to a vulnerable client. "Come on." He gently turned her toward the front doors.

Together, they started through the Great Hall. Everything had gone so smoothly that Ronin wasn't expecting the attack.

Two men rushed at them from either side. Ronin saw the glint of silver as a knife slashed at him. He shoved Peri out of the way and then felt a sharp sting on his bicep.

He blocked out the pain, already spinning, and threw up an arm to block the next blow. He jammed his forearm against the man's arm. He followed with a sharp jab to the man's ribs.

The man grunted, the knife falling to the ground. Then Ronin slammed the side of his hand against the man's throat, hard. His attacker gagged, falling to the tiles with a hand pressed to his neck.

Then Ronin heard Peri scream.

IT ALL HAPPENED SO FAST.

Peri watched as Ronin slammed into the man attacking him. He fought with quick, hard moves she could barely track.

Suddenly, a man grabbed her, wrenching her to the side. She screamed.

He spun her around. "Give it to me," he growled.

He had an accent she couldn't place, and a broad face with bushy brows. She could see Ronin was still busy fighting. People nearby were shouting and backing away.

Peri looked up at her attacker. They had to be Silk Road. The bastards holding her sister. "Please don't hurt me." Peri poured fear and panic into her voice. She did her best to look petrified.

The man relaxed a little. "Give me whatever you just collected, and you won't get hurt."

Right, and next he'd tell her he had a bridge to sell her.

As he took a menacing step closer, she struck out with her hand...and grabbed a handful of the guy's testicles.

The man gave a pained shout and his face turned gray. As he doubled over, Peri released him and then jammed her fingers into his eyes. With an agonized cry, he swung out clumsily with a fist. She didn't manage to get out of the way fast enough, and he clocked her in the face.

*Ow.* She stumbled back, pressing her palm to her cheek.

"Peri." Ronin appeared at her side. He grabbed the guy who'd hit her, slamming him into the wall.

The savage look on Ronin's face made her shiver, but

as her attacker tried to straighten, her anger spiked. She darted in and slammed her knee between the guy's legs. He moaned and slumped to the floor.

Ronin was staring at her.

She shrugged. "He made me mad."

"Remind me to stay on your good side."

That's when she saw the blood on his arm. "God, you're bleeding."

He glanced at it like it was a mosquito bite. "Nothing life-threatening." He gripped her arm and tugged her toward the entrance. The crowd stepped back to make room for them. "How about we get out of here, before we get asked questions we don't want to answer?"

They stepped outside the building, and she saw a police car pull up at the curb.

"Don't run," Ronin murmured, pulling her to the left. "We're just a normal couple out for a stroll."

She nodded, trying to calm her racing heart. Finally, they reached his bike. She saw his sleeve was soaked bright red. "You're bleeding even worse now."

He swiped at his arm. "Not much."

"Right." She pulled a bandana from her pocket and shoved his T-shirt sleeve up. "Tough guys can't admit to being injured. Goes against the code." A nasty cut had gouged his muscled bicep. It wouldn't need stitches, but could do with a proper cleaning and a bandage. She quickly tied the bandana around his arm.

"You've done that before," he said.

"Yep. And treated frostbite, set broken bones, and saved a few people from hypothermia. It's a requirement that all polar guides have advanced wilderness first aid skills."

Ronin reached out and cupped her face. His thumb stroked her cheek, and she hissed.

"That's going to bruise," he murmured.

"Well, every time I see it in the mirror, I'll remember that I knocked his balls into his throat."

Ronin winced.

Peri couldn't help but smile gingerly. "But I will 'fess up to my cheek throbbing like I got hit with a bat."

He sat on the bike. "Tough gals can admit to their injuries, huh?"

She slid on behind him. "Hell, yeah. We are way more evolved than tough guys."

He started the engine, the vibration of the bike moving up her body. As they pulled out onto the street, she held on tight to him, leaning into his body.

Her fingers brushed against hard abs, and she felt a tingle run through her body. It was probably just the aftereffects of the attack and the adrenaline. Ronin wasn't as lean and wiry as the climbers she often dated, instead he was bigger, harder, and far more intriguing.

Sitting wrapped around Ronin Cooper made her feel protected. She pressed her cheek to his back. Her parents had taught her and Amber to be self-sufficient and independent. From about the age of ten, her parents had made a game of dropping the girls in some foreign city with a train map and telling them they'd meet them at a certain location.

She'd loved her wild, adventurous childhood, but a part of her had always wondered what it was like to have your own bed, have someone bake you cookies, and to have a dog. To have someone who wanted to hold on to you, protect you, and keep you safe.

Not that Ronin was a guy who wanted to hold on. She picked up the "stay back" vibes he emanated. But something told her he was one of the good guys, even if he didn't believe it himself.

They turned onto another road, moving around a slow-moving car. The vibrations of the bike worked through her and she felt the muscles in his thighs shift as they wove their way through traffic.

What would he do if she slid her hand under his shirt and stroked his hard abs?

*Damn.* She was here to find her sister, not to fall in lust with the man helping her.

They swung into the THS parking lot, and ahead, a grim-faced Declan strode out to meet them.

## CHAPTER FOUR

---

Ronin led Peri toward the office steps with a hand to her back.

She'd fought brilliantly back at the station. Thinking of her attacking that man almost made Ronin wince again. She fought hard and dirty, and he really never wanted to be on the receiving end of it.

"You were gone for no more than thirty minutes, and there are reports of a brawl at the train station," Dec said, an eyebrow raised.

Ronin shrugged a shoulder. "They attacked first."

Dec pressed a hand to the back of his neck and exhaled loudly. "You both all right?"

"Yeah," Ronin answered.

Peri rolled her eyes. "He's bleeding. Guy caught him with a knife. He might need to see a doctor—"

Ronin scowled. "I'm not going to a doctor for a scratch."

At the top of the steps, Peri crossed her arms and rolled her eyes again. Dec looked amused.

"She got a solid blow to the face," Ronin said. "She'll need some ice for her cheek."

"I'll get the first aid kit and some ice." Dec waved them inside. "The package?"

"In the mountains," Ronin answered.

"Great. Sit down, and then we'll make a plan."

Inside THS headquarters, Ronin and Peri moved over to the conference table.

"Are you guys okay?" Darcy hurried over, worry on her pretty face.

"Fine," Ronin said.

"What did you find?" Darcy asked.

"Amber sent a package to her friend, and she had Stacey take it to a location in the mountains," Peri said. "It has to be the old cabin our grandmother left us, not far from Estes Park."

"I'll take her up there to recover it," Ronin said.

Peri flashed him a small smile and he felt a hit of warmth in his chest.

"Um, there's a short hike up to the cabin. By the time we get there, it'll be too dark to come back. The trail through there is rough and dangerous in the dark."

"You could go in the morning," Darcy suggested.

Peri bit her lip. "Silk Road wants to stop us from getting this. What if they worked out where Stacey left it? I don't want—"

Ronin grabbed her hand. "We'll go up this afternoon. We'll take sleeping bags and dinner, then come back first thing in the morning."

Relief flashed in Peri's eyes. "Thank you." Peri turned to Darcy. "Stacey said the package was post-marked Punta Arenas."

"In the very south of Chile," Darcy said.

"It's an important supply point for Antarctic expeditions, and all the bases on the western side of Antarctica," Peri murmured.

Dec reappeared and slammed an enormous first aid kit onto the table.

Peri raised a brow. "I'm guessing you guys must get hurt a lot."

"Not a lot," Dec answered.

Peri looked at Ronin. "Another tough guy." She winked.

Ronin felt the urge to laugh.

Darcy grinned at them. "There should be some ropes in there, too, so you can tie Ronin down. The man is noto-riously difficult when it comes to treating his wounds." Darcy's lips twisted. "Actually, they all are."

"Hey, any word from Burke?" Dec asked.

Darcy's nose screwed up. "He hasn't returned my call yet."

"Sit," Ronin ordered Peri.

He grabbed the ice pack from Dec and wrapped it in a kitchen towel. When he turned back to her, she was bent over, fiddling in the first aid kit.

His gaze dropped to the way her denim jeans hugged her ass. It was rounded, but toned, and just the right size to fill his hands.

*God.* He shook his head and squeezed the ice pack for a moment, tempted to press it against his crotch. She turned back to face him, and when she sat in her chair, he gently placed the ice against her face. She hissed.

"You might end up with a black eye," he said.

"Maybe. Amber gave me my first black eye. We were fighting over the incredibly cute Jimmy Summers in the eighth grade. It was one of the few years we actually attended school in the US."

"Who won?"

"It was a draw. I broke her nose, she gave me a black eye. We were both grounded, which in our family meant my parents forced us to do volunteer work at the local shelter in all our spare time. Jimmy moved on to Amanda Lewis of the big hair and developing breasts." Peri tore open a packet and pulled out an antiseptic wipe. She leaned over, shoved up his sleeve, and tore off the blood-soaked bandana. She started cleaning the cut with steady, practiced swipes.

Ronin ignored the sting. He'd lost count of how many knife wounds, bullet wounds, and dislocations he'd had treated.

"Did you have a fight over any girls when you were young?" she asked, blue gaze flicking up to his face.

"No," he answered.

She finished cleaning the cut, and then pressed a bandage over it. "Amber kissed my black eye afterward. We've always looked out for each other. My mother wasn't the kind to kiss boo-boos. She'd just tell us it was character-building." Peri's shoulders sagged. "God, I miss my sister."

Ronin lowered the ice from her cheek and grabbed

her hand. "We're going to do everything we can to bring her home."

As he watched, Peri nibbled her full lip and then straightened. She nodded. The way she pulled herself together was impressive. She looked at his wound one last time, then carefully placed the remaining gear back in the first aid kit. "Who kissed your boo-boos when you were young, Ronin?"

"No one ever kissed my boo-boos."

Her gaze shot back to his and he saw the questions swimming in them. Not that he intended to answer. He looked away. Pity was the one thing he'd never wanted and never needed.

She moved closer. When he looked back, he saw the top of her copper-colored head, as she pressed a featherlight kiss to the bandage on his arm.

Something moved through him and he just stared at her. She looked up and their gazes locked. Ronin's senses filled with Peri. The bright, sunshine smell of her, the warmth of her body, the sweetness of her face.

"Ronin, I don't know you very well, but I..."

He just kept staring at her.

She shot him a self-deprecating smile. "You'll soon learn that I have a habit of just blurting things out. I don't play games or put on pretenses. Growing up all around the world meant I learned to be upfront."

"Peri—"

"I really want to kiss you," she said quickly.

Damn, she was making this hard on him. "Peri."

"I know that tone." She tried to pull away.

He should have let her go, let the moment slip away, but for some reason, Ronin held on tight.

"It's okay," she hurried on. "You're not attracted to me, I get it."

"I am attracted to you." He almost winced at the deep growl of his voice.

She tugged her hand. "You don't have to say that—"

He tugged her forward until their lips brushed. Just a quick graze that gave him the briefest taste of her.

She blinked, her gaze dropping to his lips.

"You're a client—"

She arched a brow. "That's a lame excuse, Ronin. I know your boss married a client."

"I'm not a nice guy, Peri. I've been places and done things you couldn't imagine."

"We all have, Ronin. It doesn't mean we can't do better, or want different things for our lives."

"Not a home kind of guy. I've never had one, or at least, not a good one. I'm best when I'm on the move, and I'm best working in the dark, doing the jobs no one else wants to do."

Her gaze scanned his face. "Maybe you just haven't tried the light? Besides, none of that means you have to be alone."

"I'll never have a home, a picket fence, or a dog." For the first time in his life, he regretted it. "Sounds like you deserve all those things." He stood. "I'm going to pick up my truck and make some plans with Dec. Silk Road is watching us. We need to make sure they don't follow us into the mountains."

RONIN GLANCED in the rearview mirror, but didn't see anyone tailing them as they followed the highway up into the Rocky Mountains.

Five vehicles had headed out of the THS office parking lot with Ronin, Dec, Logan, Cal, and Hale Carter behind the wheels. They'd all taken circuitous routes through Denver to lose anyone who was following them. Peri had stayed hidden until he'd given her the all clear as he'd left Denver behind.

Now she sat beside him, staring out the window. The road was lined with lush trees bursting with green.

"So your grandmother lived up here?" he asked. "That why you picked Denver to live?"

Peri nodded. "Mom and Dad dumped Amber and me on Gram at least once a year. She was a kooky old lady and I loved her. My grandpa died when my mom was little, but she told me Gram made a good life for them." Peri smiled. "I loved her and the mountains. The scenery, scrambling through the trees with Amber, Gram baking us cookies. I even climbed for the first time up here. There's just something about the mountains that inspires awe and peace."

He stared at the mountain view ahead. It was breathtaking, and he understood what she meant.

"So, do you miss being a Navy SEAL?" she asked.

Ronin's hands flexed on the wheel. "No. Working for THS means less flying bullets." Usually.

"When I researched THS, I saw you'd worked for the CIA, as well."

"Yes." When he didn't say anything else, he felt her looking at him, and he gripped the wheel.

"Don't worry, Ronin. You don't want to talk about it, you don't have to."

When he looked back at her, she was looking out the window again. She didn't seem upset. He'd had more than a few women get testy when he refused to share his past with them.

They continued on and passed through the mountain town of Estes Park. He knew it was a base for anyone heading into Rocky Mountain National Park, and its main street was filled with shops, restaurants, and galleries. It was busy all year round.

Soon, they turned onto a smaller road, and then a smaller dirt track, heading up a hill. When she told him to pull over by a dilapidated gate with peeling white paint, he knew they only had about an hour of sunlight left.

"We haven't maintained the road," she said. "I want to renovate the cabin, but I've been busy with my gym and my house."

They climbed out and pulled on their backpacks. Ronin followed Peri through the gate and they started the hike up to the cabin. The ground was rough and rutted. The track needed a hell of a lot of maintenance, and Peri was right. This would be a difficult hike in the dark.

Almost an hour passed, and then they cleared the trees, and the view even made Ronin's jaded senses pause to take it all in. The golden-orange light of the setting sun drenched the valley. Trees swept down the mountain and he drew in a deep breath, pulling in the scent of the trees.

"Pretty special, huh?" Peri said.

He glanced at her and saw her face was the most relaxed it had been since he'd first spotted her across a crowded wedding reception. "Yeah. Very special."

A flush of pink heated her cheeks and she looked back at the scenery. "Just being here, breathing in the fresh mountain air, does something to still the soul."

Ronin wasn't sure he wanted to still his soul, or listen to what it had to say. "It'll be dark soon. Let's get to the cabin and find this package."

She nodded and pointed. That's when he noticed the cabin nestled among the trees. It was a simple structure made of logs with a deck at the front with a few solid wooden chairs. It had a dilapidated air, but good bones.

Peri jogged up the steps and pushed open the unlocked door. Inside, the living area wasn't big, the kitchen was postage-stamp sized, and he saw three doors for the two bedrooms and bathroom.

"It's a bit dusty in here." Peri moved over to a table, dumped her backpack, and pulled an oil lantern into the center of the table. She flicked it on and it cast a golden glow through the room. "Amber came and stayed up here not too long ago. She said she'd stocked up the oil and wood for the fire."

Mention of her sister made worry cross Peri's face. Then she squared her shoulders and marched to the nearest door. When she opened it, Ronin saw a small bedroom with two single beds.

Peri smiled. "This was our room. Gram always put matching pink covers on our beds, which we both hated." The hated covers were long gone now, the mattresses stripped bare. She moved to the center of the room and pressed down with her boot.

The wooden floorboard squeaked.

She knelt down and pried it up. "Our secret hiding place." She reached under the board. She pulled her hand out and held up a small, red carabiner. She smiled again. "This was from the first time I went climbing. Gram organized it with the son of a friend of hers. He was in his twenties and had his hands full teaching two teenage girls who were crushing on him." She set the carabiner aside. Next, she pulled out a folded piece of paper. She flicked it open and pain spasmed on her face.

He took in the loopy writing and decided it didn't belong to Peri.

"Amber's," Peri said. "Describing being completely in love with a boy staying in a cabin down the road one summer." Next, Peri pulled up a small, sealed envelope. Her fingers clenched on it.

"Peri?"

"I'm okay." She tore it open. A small black thumb drive fell onto her palm. "This is it."

But what it held exactly would have to wait until they got back to Denver. Unable to stop himself, he reached out and grabbed Peri's hand. "This is one step closer to finding your sister."

---

DARCY SAT in the now-quiet warehouse, enjoying the peace, and checking some deep-level searches she had running. Some of them were...not quite legal.

Everyone had headed home for the evening. Everyone had someone to head home with except her.

Ignoring the pang in her chest, Darcy patted the side of her sleek screen. Her computer system was all she needed to keep herself challenged and entertained. Well, that and her well-endowed vibrator at home by her bed.

With a grin, she pulled out her phone, but her smile turned to a frown. Still no call from Special Agent "I'm in charge and I'll never let you forget it." She'd left the man three messages. The asshole was avoiding her.

She glanced at her slim, silver watch. It was late in DC, but something told her he'd still be at the office. She dragged her chair closer to her computer and got to work, her fingers flying.

Darcy loved computers. It didn't mean she didn't like people, but there was something so right about the programming. Everything was logical and under her control.

*Ah-ha*. She studied the information on her screen. She could see a certain FBI agent was still logged on. She paused. This was highly illegal. The FBI really didn't like people hacking into their system. She pursed her lips. Then again, Burke had hacked her system more than once. She might not have an entire team of tech geniuses at her fingertips like he did, but she was more than capable of hacking into the FBI without anyone noticing.

Darcy leaned over her keyboard. A moment later, she barely resisted a fist pump. *Yes*. An image of Special Agent Alastair Burke appeared on her screen.

He was sitting at his desk, frowning at some paperwork. He hadn't noticed the camera on his laptop turn on, and she had a second to just look at him. So serious. He had a not-quite handsome face. It was a little too hard and focused to be handsome.

But damn, the man drew the eye. He might drive her crazy, but add in a body she knew he kept honed to hard precision, and the suit, and the gun holster...

"Darcy? What the hell?" He was looking right at her, a frown on his face.

She straightened. "You didn't return my calls."

"So you hacked the FBI?"

How dare he sound so shocked. "You hack my system all the time!"

He muttered a curse and rose. She got a good view of a white shirt—still crisp because she was certain Burke intimidated even shirt wrinkles—tucked into dark trousers, and that pistol in its holster. She cleared her throat, and watched him close his office door before he sat again.

"Don't get caught," he growled. "I'm not saving your pretty ass if you end up in a cell."

Were FBI agents allowed to say ass? *Wait.* He'd noticed her *ass.* Some sensation flicked through Darcy before she stomped down on it. No. Nope. Hell nope. She wasn't going there.

"We have a mission." There, her tone was appropriately business-like. "I was hoping to get some information from you—"

"I don't have anything to give you."

She narrowed her gaze. "Burke, I'm about to send my brother and friends to Antarctica—"

"Antarctica?" A muscle in his jaw jumped. "Tell Dec not to go."

"Our client's sister got lured there by Silk Road. She's missing and her life is in danger. We don't stand by and let innocent people get hurt and killed by these bastards. And last time I checked, neither do you."

"Dammit." He shoved a hand through his dark hair. "I have no jurisdiction in Antarctica, Darcy. But I've heard some chatter about something going on there. There are players involved above my pay grade."

*Damn.* That didn't sound good. "Can you give me anything?"

"No."

"Please." Anything could help keep Dec and the others alive. "I'd consider it a personal favor."

He stared at her, and she found herself caught by deep green eyes.

"I'll owe you," she added quietly. Dec had just gotten married, and was in love and happy. Logan was head over heels for Sydney. And Ronin watched Peri Butler in a way Darcy had never seen him look at a woman before. She wanted them all home safe from this mission.

Burke's gaze sharpened. "*You'll* owe me. Not Declan. Not THS."

Her heart gave a hard knock. Why did she suddenly feel like she was dancing with the devil and signing her soul over? "Deal."

"Tell Dec not to go." Burke sighed, like he knew that was never going to happen. "There has been lots of Silk Road chatter about a top-secret mission to Antarctica. My team handed everything over...to another team."

"The mysterious team in black with drones, who shoot first and ask questions later?"

"They're the good guys."

"Sure."

"Another top Silk Road leader is said to be involved, Darcy. You tell Dec to be prepared for *anything*." Burke leaned his forearms on his desk, his gaze intense. "I'll warn any friendlies involved that THS has a team on the ground."

That was something, at least. Allies were always welcome. "See. That wasn't too hard. You should have just returned my calls."

"If you're looking for a man to be at your beck and call, Darcy, that isn't me."

No, Alastair Burke had bossy, authoritative, and alpha male stamped all over him. He was nothing like the charming, successful businessmen she dated. She gave him a smile. "No man has ever complained."

Something flashed in his gaze and his voice lowered. "Don't push me, Darcy."

All of a sudden, she felt like she'd stepped onto boggy ground. "Well, now that you've hacked my system and I've hacked yours, we're even. You stay away from my computers and I'll stay away from yours."

A faint smile tilted his firm lips. "We'll see. Goodnight, Darcy."

"Goodnight, Agent Burke."

"And don't forget...you owe me." The screen went blank.

*Ooh.* Darcy poked her tongue out at the empty screen. The man always had to have the last word.

## CHAPTER FIVE

P eri sat in one of the chairs on the deck, her legs tucked up beneath her, munching on her sandwich.

Night had fallen, and she was enjoying listening to the night-time quiet and looking at the amazing sweep of stars that filled the sky. They were so breathtaking.

She wondered if Amber was looking up at the stars. Peri felt a spear of pain in her chest. The small thumb drive was a heavy weight in Peri's pocket and she desperately wanted to know what was on it.

Beside her, Ronin sat quietly in his chair. The silence wasn't uncomfortable. She liked that he didn't feel the need to fill the silence with talk. He had this quiet core of steel she liked a lot.

"Thank you for helping me," she said.

"No need to thank me. It's my job."

His job. Right. "I feel silly now that I spied on you and your friends."

"When it comes to Silk Road, it makes sense not to

trust." In the faint light from the window, his eyes looked even darker than usual. "And like I told you, you shouldn't trust me."

He just felt the need to keep warning her off him. "Do you warn all women away?"

His mouth morphed into a scowl.

Hmm, Peri didn't think many women called him on his dark moodiness. They were probably already scared off by the dangerous look on his face. But Peri was made of sterner stuff. She took another bite of her sandwich, chewed, and swallowed. "So you're too big, bad, and dangerous?"

He sent her a sharp look and the scowl deepened.

Peri fought back a smile. "I grew up seeing some of the shadiest, most dangerous backstreets around the world." Traveling to so many countries meant she'd had a few close shaves. "Sorry, but you aren't big, bad, and dark, Ronin. You're barely gray."

He blinked.

"You fought for your country, and dedicated your life to protecting it. I don't know what you did for the CIA, and I can see it scarred you, but you were fighting for the good guys."

"Sometimes the good guys have to do bad things."

The buried pain in his voice hurt her heart. "That doesn't make you bad, though."

They sat there in the darkness for a while, the quiet broken by some small animal rustling in the bushes nearby.

"Are you from Denver?" she asked.

"No."

She stifled a sigh. Clearly, this was another topic that was closed to discussion.

"New York," he said abruptly.

"Really? Do you have family there?"

"I have no idea. I was abandoned as a newborn in an alley. I was wrapped in a blanket and drug addicted."

She sucked in a sharp breath. His tone was monotone, emotionless. "I'm sorry—"

"Nothing for you to be sorry about." He rubbed the back of his neck and looked a little surprised he was even talking at all. "It's an ugly story and in the past."

Except it wasn't. Peri could tell it wasn't.

He stood abruptly. "I want to do a lap of the cabin before we go to sleep."

She sat up. "You think Silk Road could have followed us?"

"I doubt it. But I never take chances."

Of course, he didn't. He was the man doing security checks in the dark so others could sleep safely. She grabbed her pocket and felt the slight weight of the thumb drive in there.

Ronin reached out and touched her cheek. A featherlight touch. "Stay strong. Your sister left you a clue so we could find her."

Throat tight, Peri nodded. He pulled back and for a second, she missed his touch. She felt such a pull toward this man. He was like a black hole—mysterious, dangerous, and inexorable.

"Goodnight, Peri." He turned and disappeared into the darkness.

PERI WOKE WITH A START.

She almost rolled right off the narrow, single bed before she caught herself. The dark was thick and impenetrable, and it took her a second to remember where she was.

Gram's cabin. Amber's thumb drive. Ronin.

She heard another noise. A deep masculine growl. She sat up and reached under her pillow, pulling out the thumb drive. She stuck it in the waistband of her yoga leggings, since she was braless under her loose tank top and had no pockets. She climbed out of bed and heard a harsh sound from the neighboring bedroom.

She frowned. It sounded like Ronin was having a nightmare.

She tiptoed toward the other room, glad she knew the cabin layout in her head. When she reached the room, moonlight cast a glow over the double bed. Ronin was shirtless, thrashing under his light sleeping bag.

"No!" he called out. "Bastards."

Peri moved closer to the bed, and wasn't sure if she should touch him. She saw his muscles were bunched.

"Ronin—"

He leaped off the bed and took her down. It happened so fast and as her back hit the floorboards, the air rushed out of her. His heavy weight landed on top of her, pinning her to the floor.

She looked up and could just make out his glittering, wild eyes.

She sucked in a breath. "Ronin." She tried to keep her voice calm. "It's Peri."

He froze. "Peri?"

"Yes. You were...dreaming." Or having a hellacious nightmare.

Some of the tension drained out of him. "Peri."

"That's me." She reached up and ran a hand over his dark hair. He kept it short, but what was there was thick and silky. "You're okay now."

"Shit, I'm sorry. You shouldn't have come in here. I could have hurt you."

"In case you haven't noticed, I'm not scared of you."

She felt his gaze move over her face. "You should be."

Then he leaned down and shocked her by fusing his mouth to hers.

*Oh. God.* Heat flooded Peri and as her mouth parted, he plundered. The hot shock of his tongue thrust into her mouth—taking and tasting. A spear of heat shot through her and she stroked his tongue with hers.

Moaning, she slid her hands into his hair. His body felt so big and hard against hers. Oh, boy, the man could kiss. He did it with the same focused intensity he did everything else.

She pushed and they rolled across the floor until they hit the edge of the bed. Ronin groaned and they rolled again. Peri ended up on top and she dug her legs against his hips. She pressed her palms against his bare chest, feeling the heat of his taut skin and the hard muscles beneath.

He jerked and rolled her again. This time Peri found herself pinned by his body, his lean hips falling into the cradle of hers. A very hard cock covered only by soft gym shorts pressed between her legs. Peri moaned again, her nails digging into his scalp as she deepened the kiss. She wanted more, anything, everything.

A beeping sound broke through the fiery haze of need.

Ronin tore his mouth off hers with a curse. Then he jackknifed off her and snatched up his phone from the bedside table.

Peri sat up, pushing her hair back off her face, and trying to calm her out-of-control hormones. "What is it?"

He uttered another curse, staring at his phone. "When I did my walkaround earlier, I set up some small infrared cameras outside."

Of course, he did. She guessed the soldier and agent could leave the service, but it never left him. "And?"

He yanked a shirt over his head and started pulling his shoes on. "Get some shoes on and make sure you have the drive." He tilted his phone at her.

Peri instantly saw the converging colored blobs and her heart kicked against her ribs.

"There's a team of seven moving in to surround the cabin. We have to go. Now."

---

AS SOON AS Ronin's boots hit the ground, he reached up and helped Peri out of the window.

He pressed his mouth to her ear. "Stay quiet and head straight into the trees." He gripped her hand and together they jogged from the cabin.

He had his Glock tucked in his waistband, but he was hoping they could use the cover of darkness to avoid their visitors. How the hell had Silk Road found them? There must have been a tracking device on his vehicle. He ground his teeth together. He should have checked.

But right now, he needed to focus on keeping Peri safe.

"What's the plan?" she whispered.

"Get away from here. Then find a way back to Denver. Even if we can get back to my truck, they've likely already disabled it."

"Can't you get a message to Dec?"

"No signal. Silk Road is jamming it."

Peri muttered some interesting curses under her breath and despite their situation, Ronin found himself fighting back a smile.

"There's a climbable cliff face a little farther to the west," she said. "It's doable with no gear, if you know it."

"And you know it."

"Hell, yeah." Her tone turned dry. "Although I've never tried it in my pajamas, with no bra on, in the dark."

Ronin jerked to a halt. "You aren't wearing a bra." Images started running through his head.

"That's the bit you heard?" There was humor in her voice. "Such a man."

"I am a man."

But the sounds of voices not too far away had him refocusing. He tugged her onward and picked up speed. Branches slapped at his face.

"Here," she whispered.

The trees cleared and they reached a rocky ridge. In the moonlight, he saw the cliff face below them.

"There's a huge diagonal crack that runs down it." Peri crouched, the moonlight making her bare shoulders gleam. "There are lots of decent hand and footholds around it."

Her tone had turned brisk and no-nonsense. Ronin knew he was seeing a glimpse of the climbing instructor and expedition guide.

"Take your time," she added. "Test each grip. We don't have gear, so there is no margin for error."

"Got it." He watched her lower one foot over the edge. "Peri?" When she looked up, he pressed a quick, firm kiss to her lips. "Be careful."

She nodded and started climbing down. Ronin set his boot into a crack and followed.

They moved down carefully and steadily. He saw that Peri had relaxed a little. She was in her element and she'd probably forgotten about the people above searching for them. She moved with ease, and a sure athletic grace. Even in the dark, he could tell she was a hell of a climber.

Suddenly, voices sounded directly overhead.

"Fuck. Colston will have our asses."

"They can't have gone far."

Ronin paused and looked up. He saw flashlights bobbing. Just a little below him, Peri froze. Damn, if the bastards looked straight down, they'd spot him and Peri.

He moved, climbing down to Peri's level. He covered her body with his, offering what protection he could, and pressed her against the rock.

One flashlight arced downward, just a few feet from them. He heard Peri's fast breathing.

"We're fine," he murmured against her ear. So many times he'd been hidden, waiting to see if he'd be discovered by the enemy. "Think of a situation that makes you feel good."

"Kissing you."

He stilled. *Hell.* "Something that won't give me a hard on in a dangerous situation."

A near-soundless giggle. Then she wiggled her butt.

Ronin nuzzled her neck. "Stop it. Time to get moving again, because they're gone."

"Gone?" She looked up. "Right. Bad guys are gone."

He smiled. "Come on. Let's get off this rock face." He forced himself away from her body, telling himself that he didn't miss the contact.

It took them a few more minutes to navigate down the rest of the cliff.

At the bottom, Peri dusted off her hands. "So, what now?"

"Can we get to a main road from here?" he asked.

She nodded. "We can get back to where we came in. It's a short hike but you know it's rough. We'll have to go slowly."

"Well, these bastards hiked in to surprise us..."

She perked up. "So they left vehicles somewhere."

He nodded.

"Sneaky." Her teeth were bright in the darkness. "I like it. I hope you can hotwire a car."

They started off through the trees. "Standard secret agent skill."

A startled laugh. "Did you just make a joke?"

"Maybe." God, no other woman had ever made him want to smile so much before.

"I like you, Ronin Cooper."

With that admission, she forged ahead. Ronin followed. He liked her too. And he had no idea what the hell he was going to do about it.

## CHAPTER SIX

When Peri and Ronin pulled into the THS parking lot in their borrowed Silk Road vehicle, dawn was only just lighting the eastern horizon in streaks of pink and gold. The warehouse was ablaze with lights, so she guessed the team was awake and doing their thing.

All the adrenaline of their escape was long gone and Peri had managed to doze on the ride back. She rubbed her bare arms and then touched her hair. She stifled a groan. It was a hopelessly tangled rat's nest.

They walked up the steps to the building and that's when she realized Ronin wasn't wearing any socks with his shoes. She was still in her pajamas and braless. They looked like survivors of a shipwreck. He held the door and waved her inside.

"What the fuck?" Dec appeared. "I got your message an hour ago. Are you two okay?"

"No thanks to Silk Road," Ronin said darkly.

"Oh, my God." Darcy stepped up beside her brother. "You guys look terrible."

"Silk Road sent a team in to take the thumb drive," Ronin said.

"We decided to leave," Peri said. "And climb down a cliff face in the dark. In our pajamas."

"We need to check all THS vehicles," Ronin said. "They must have tracking devices."

Dec nodded. "On it. And I'll send Hale and Cal up to the cabin to get your truck and gear."

Darcy waved an arm at Peri. "Come on. We'll head upstairs and get you in a hot shower. I'm sure Layne will have some clothes that will fit you."

Peri groaned. "A hot shower sounds like heaven." She looked at Ronin.

"I have some spare gear in my locker and we have showers down here." He reached out and squeezed her shoulder. "I'll see you soon."

Conscious that Dec and Darcy were watching them with raised eyebrows, Peri swiveled and held her hand out to Darcy. "I'm guessing you'll want this." The thumb drive rested on her palm.

"You found it." Darcy took it, an eager light in her eyes. "I'll see what's on here."

Peri took her time in the shower, and after working all the tangles out of her hair, she wasn't even too weirded out by borrowing Layne Ward's bra and clothes, which thankfully were dark green cargo pants and a T-shirt with the pyramid-shaped Treasure Hunter Security logo on it. The archeologist had been so gracious setting out clothes, towels, and toiletries for Peri in her sleek, spacious apartment above the THS offices.

When Peri came downstairs, she saw Darcy moving between two computers, Dec and Logan leaning over maps on the table, and Ronin sitting nearby cradling a mug of coffee. His hair was damp and he was wearing a clean set of clothes.

"Hey," he said.

She smiled. "I feel human again." She noticed a few scratches on his cheek and reached out to touch them. "What happened here?"

"Tree branches during our mad dash. It's nothing. I've had far, far worse."

She bet he had. On his SEAL missions and whatever undercover assignments he'd done for the CIA. Whatever he'd done for them had left him with vicious nightmares and the belief he had to hold himself apart from others. Even here with his friends, he somehow held himself off to the side.

Everyone needed someone. Peri had come into the world connected to another being who'd been a part of everything in her life. Amber might drive her nuts sometimes, but she never doubted her sister's love and loyalty.

Ronin had come into the world with no one. Not even the mother who'd birthed him.

A part of Peri wanted to show him that he could have more in his life if he just let people in, and let her closer. Something also told her that would require patience, stubbornness, and sheer grit.

She leaned down and pressed a kiss to the scratches.

His dark eyes were locked on her and she saw so much shift through them, even though he stayed motionless.

The click of heels shattered the moment. Darcy appeared, excitement on her face. "I got the data off the drive."

Peri spun. "Really?"

"It's data on the expedition to Antarctica," Darcy said. "Maps, itineraries, notes."

Peri rubbed her hands up and down her arms, feeling cold. Dec and Logan had straightened, both standing with arms crossed over their chests and staring up at Darcy's wall of screens.

Darcy pointed. "The maps here show the location of the pyramid. In the notes, I see they were planning to fly into a seasonal camp. It would have been closed down a few months back." Darcy's elegant fingers flew over her keyboard.

Peri tried to focus on all the information, but all she could think about was Amber. Was she okay?

A hand touched her shoulder and squeezed. She looked up and saw Ronin wasn't looking at her, but he'd still sensed she was upset. *Focus on your sister, and not the sexy man beside you.*

"After the pyramid was first discovered, Silk Road sent a very small recon team in. It looks like they did some drilling in the ice near the pyramid." Then Darcy gasped.

"What did they find?" Dec demanded.

His sister raised her head. "They hit metal."

"How is this possible?" Ronin said. "It's been covered with ice for *millions* of years."

"That may not be exactly correct," a deep, male voice interjected.

Everyone turned, and Peri watched a good-looking man stride in. He had a tanned, handsome face, and a wide, charming smile. The tall woman beside him moved with an athletic stride. Her short, dark hair suited her tough face, and she looked like she could take every man in the room down and not break a sweat doing it.

The woman stopped and pressed her hands to her hips. "You had to call me in on my days off?"

"I actually called Zach, not you," Dec said.

The woman snorted. "Since I was *busy* with Zach, you call him in, you call me in."

Ah, so the man who looked like a handsome adventurer who should be hacking vines off ancient jungle temples, or dusting sand off buried tombs, was Dr. Zachariah James. That made the woman Morgan Kincaid, one of THS's best security specialists.

"Zach and Morgan, this is Peri Butler," Ronin said.

Peri shook hands with the couple. "Nice to meet you."

"I hear your sister got mixed up with Silk Road and is missing," Zach said. "I'm sorry to hear that."

Peri inclined her head. "Thanks for helping." She glanced at Morgan. "Sorry to ruin your days off."

Morgan waved a hand. "Your sister needs help, and to be fair, any time I can help ruin Silk Road's day is a good one."

"I'm not sure what I can do, but I'll do anything to help," Zach said. "I've unfortunately seen what Silk Road is capable of. I hope Dec, Ronin, and the others help you find your sister."

They all sat down around the conference table. Zach stood at the head, talking quietly with Darcy as she tapped on her tablet.

"So, Silk Road, led by Peri's sister, Amber, has gone to Antarctica, and not returned," Darcy said.

Morgan was still standing and leaned a hip against the table. "What the hell is in Antarctica that would interest Silk Road? They going after penguins, now?"

Zach shoved his hands in the pockets of his jeans. "Darcy tells me Layne mentioned a link with the Nazis and Antarctica. She's correct. Hitler was very interested in Antarctica. There were rumors that the Nazis were planning on building, or possibly even did build, a secret base there."

"A base in Antarctica?" Dec shook his head. "Doesn't sound credible."

Zach smiled. "Did you know that just last year, Russian scientists discovered a secret, abandoned Nazi base in the Arctic?"

"What?" Peri breathed.

"It was set up on an island, ostensibly to gather strategic weather reports. But from the items and preserved papers recovered, it appears the Germans called the base Treasure Hunter."

Silence filled the room.

"You think they were really on the hunt for ancient artifacts?" Ronin said.

Zach shrugged. "I don't know for sure, but it seems highly likely."

"Okay…" Peri said slowly. "And you said they wanted to build a base in Antarctica, too? To find artifacts?"

"Artifacts of power. It was an obsession of Hitler's. He wanted to find powerful artifacts and then use them to create weapons to win the war."

"Artifacts of power?" She looked around the table, but no one seemed surprised by Zach's declaration. "There's nothing in Antarctica but ice."

Zach smiled again. "I specialize in megalithic cultures. The cultures that built vast temples and structures with large blocks of stone. They left behind ruins like Stonehenge, the megalithic temples on Malta, Göbekli Tepe in Turkey, just to name a few. There are megalithic structures all across the globe. It's my belief that there were advanced cultures that were destroyed by floods at the end of the last ice age."

Shock reverberated through Peri's body. "Are you talking about *Atlantis*? Atlantis isn't real."

"Not the mythical Atlantis," Zach said. "But the civilization that probably spawned the myth."

Peri looked around the room. No one looked shocked.

Morgan nodded. "We've seen some of the artifacts they've left behind. We can't conclusively prove that they are advanced technology, but they are something."

"Generally, what we've found has been appropriated by the government," Dec said with a growl.

"He means taken," Darcy added.

"By government agencies that don't even have names," Dec finished.

Peri looked up at Ronin and he nodded.

"Okay," Peri said. "Even if I wanted to believe that

there were pre-flood civilizations with advanced technologies, and that Hitler, and now Silk Road were after any artifacts left behind, it doesn't change the fact that Antarctica has been covered by ice for millions of years. No civilization could have built anything there."

"Well, that may not be true," Zach said, pressing his hands against the table. "First, I need to tell you about a map. The Piri Reis map."

"What is it?" Peri asked.

"It is a world map made by an Ottoman general in 1513," Zach said.

"I'll get an image up on the screen," Darcy said.

"And?" Peri prompted.

"It shows the coastline of Antarctica...without its ice sheet on it."

---

THERE WAS silence in the room. Ronin studied the map Darcy had put up on the screen, unable to believe it. It looked old, with sailing ships drawn on it crossing the oceans, and lines radiating out across the parchment.

"Piri Reis apparently used older maps he'd acquired to compile his map," Zach said. "Which suggests that the Antarctic coastline was mapped, without ice, sometime during human history."

"If that was true, how could any ruins or artifacts have survived?" Peri said. "They'd have been ground away beneath all that ice."

"Now, there's a theory," Zach said. "It's called crustal displacement theory. Many people believe it's impossible, and I'm not sure I subscribe to it, myself. The idea is that some force can cause the crust of the Earth to shift in a large piece."

Ronin frowned. "So what you're saying is, the Antarctic land mass was likely once located farther north, and a part of it was free of ice, but crustal displacement moved it down to the pole, and the land iced over?"

"Exactly," Zach said. "Proponents of the theory say the last crustal displacement happened at the end of the last ice age."

Peri shook her head. "What could cause that?"

"No one knows," Zach conceded. "A large meteorite impact, forces in the crust, something unknown. Someone theorized the mass of the polar ice itself could force the shift, but that's been disproven. Some people believe crustal displacement also explains the existence of animals like wooly mammoths that have been found frozen in ice...but with their stomachs full of just-eaten foods from a more temperate climate."

"If this theory is true," Dec said. "You're telling me a part of Antarctica was free of ice about what, 11,000 years ago?"

"Yes. And it was likely mapped by the civilization that called it home."

Peri stood up, her chair scraping on the floor. "And that advanced civilization built cities there, and possibly left technology behind that Silk Road is after?"

Zach nodded. "That's what I'm telling you."

"What do you make of this, Zach?" Darcy nodded toward the screen that currently displayed the image of the pyramid protruding from the snow.

The archeologist strode up close to the image, his gaze narrowed as he studied the image.

"It could be manmade," he said. "Pyramids are a common structure that have been built by civilizations all across the globe. Egypt, Mexico, China, Indonesia, Peru, Spain, even out in the Pacific islands. This could be the remnants of an advanced civilization in Antarctica."

Darcy swiveled. "I've got some more of the information. Based on the notes on Amber's thumb drive, I've confirmed that the Silk Road team flew from Punta Arenas to the currently abandoned Unity Camp at Union Glacier. It's only active in the warmer months and finishes up by the end of January."

"So it's been empty for several months," Ronin said.

"Yes. Now isn't the ideal time for expeditions to Antarctica. The temperatures are falling, and the hours of light each day are dropping."

Dec crossed his arms. "They landed at Unity, and from there, they would have headed straight for the pyramid."

Peri dragged in a breath. "I don't care what crazy theory Silk Road has, or what the hell they want to find, I just want to find my sister."

"I know." Dec's gaze met Ronin's. "We'll start planning a trip to go in after them."

Ronin saw Peri's chest hitch. He realized she'd been worried they wouldn't go. He touched her arm. "We'll get down there and find her."

"I'm making plans now," Darcy said with a reassuring smile. "Luckily for us, Dec has a friend who runs a research station not too far from the pyramid location."

Dec groaned. "Dr. Melinda Browning. She's...a character."

"She's an Australian scientist, and she's spent years down in Antarctica," Darcy said. "Mel's friends with our parents. She runs the Aurora Station, which is jointly run by Australia, Sweden, and Chile. It's on the Chilean claim, but many of its supplies come via Australia."

"Patch me through to her," Dec said.

"I will." Darcy tucked some hair behind her ear. "There was one more thing in the information from your sister."

Ronin sensed something in Darcy's tone and saw Peri tense.

"What?" Peri asked.

"It was a note she'd typed in a document. She was clearly interrupted writing it." Darcy's blue-gray gaze swung around the room. "She says that Silk Road is after a weapon."

Peri gasped and Ronin ground his teeth together.

"Fuck," Dec bit out. "As if things weren't bad enough."

"Any other information?" Ronin asked. "A description of this weapon? Or what it does?"

Darcy shook her head.

"This doesn't change anything. Darce," Dec said. "Contact Aurora Station. Everyone, get to work, we have a mission to plan."

As everyone split off to plan the trip, Ronin saw Peri spin and stalk over to the windows. She stood there, staring out at the Denver skyline. The morning sun lit her hair up and he wasn't sure he'd ever seen a woman look so beautiful.

Nearby, Ronin heard Morgan laugh. A sound that was perilously close to a giggle. He shook his head. Morgan was the toughest woman he knew, and one of the few people he wanted beside him in a firefight. He'd never believed that Morgan would find a man who'd take the sharpness off her edges, but clearly, Zach was that man.

He watched Morgan lean into Zach. Their closeness just underscored how alone Peri looked.

Ronin had rescued a lot of people in his lifetime, but he'd rarely hugged them, offered them comfort, or had the right words to help make them feel better. He knew he should stay away from Peri.

A few seconds passed, and then he headed over to her.

## CHAPTER SEVEN

P eri stared out the window at the Denver skyline. The sound of the THS team talking behind her, discussing and planning, was an indeterminate rumble of noise in her ears.

She'd made a life here in Denver, was making a home. But if she lost her twin, the other part of her, something would always be missing. Her chest felt so tight it hurt.

She sensed a presence behind her and knew instantly it was Ronin.

"Silk Road must have found something down there," she said.

"Yes."

"And they aren't going to let my sister walk away. Not if she's seen this weapon."

"No."

*God.* He didn't mince words. Right now, she both

liked and hated that about him. She stared at their faint reflection in the glass. "Do you think she's still alive?"

"There's a chance." He spun her to face him. "And while there's a chance, there's hope. If they found the weapon, we would have heard something. My guess? They're likely still down there searching, and need her help."

She wondered if he truly believed that. A sense of determination flared in her. She *wasn't* giving up on her sister. "We're going to find her. And I'm going to make the people holding her pay."

"Get over here, you two," Dec called out. "Planning update."

They all circled around the table. It was covered in a mass of papers and a tablet. Dec pressed his palms against the table, his gaze running over the group. "I got a message through to Melinda. She'll help us out."

"When do we go?" Peri asked.

"I'll lead the team," Dec said. "We'll keep it small. Peri, Logan, and Ronin will come, too."

Logan made a grumpy sound. "I hate the snow and the cold."

Peri saw everyone around the table roll their eyes, so she guessed this was usual operating procedure for Logan. "Gear and supplies?"

"I'll arrange for supplies," Darcy said. "We can get some things in Punta Arenas. Melinda will supply the snowmobiles. You must have your own full set of expedition gear, Peri?"

Peri nodded.

"Well, head home and pack," Darcy said. "I'm

arranging flights to Chile now. From Punta Arenas, I'll arrange for you to catch the regular cargo flight to Aurora Station."

"Ronin, you take Peri to her place," Dec said. "Silk Road has come after her twice, so be careful."

Everything turned into a whirlwind of action after that. Peri let Ronin usher her out to a huge, black truck—which apparently belonged to Logan—and help her into the passenger seat.

She'd been so alone with her worry about Amber, and now she was surrounded by these big, tough people willing to help her. Her belly quivered, and she glanced his way as he started the truck. She liked it. She liked him.

"Where to?"

She told him her address, and before she knew it, they were pulling up in front of her little house near Wash Park.

She knew it needed renovating, but it had good bones. Every time she saw it, a part of her sighed. It was cute and it was hers. The fence was rotted, the porch was sagging, and the paint was peeling, but it was all hers.

"I sunk a chunk of my savings into my gym and the house," she said, as she led him up the path. "I'm renovating this place one project at a time."

"What about your gym?" he asked. "Can you afford to be away from it?"

She nodded. "I have a great manager and a brilliant team. They'll run just fine without me."

When she went to open the front door, he stopped her. "Let me check the place out first. Stay here."

She watched as he pulled what looked like a Glock from the holster on his side. He opened the door and slipped inside like a stealthy shadow.

Peri waited for him to come back. As the minutes ticked by, her muscles tightened. What if he'd run into trouble? What if he needed help? Screw this. It wasn't in her nature to wait. She'd just pulled the door open, when he reappeared, sliding his gun back into the holster.

His dark gaze narrowed. "What the hell do you think you're doing?"

"It took so long, I thought you might need help."

He gave her a strange look, and shook his head. "When I tell you to stay somewhere, you stay there."

She snapped a salute at him. "Yes, sir."

"I can hear the sarcasm."

"Smart man." She brushed past him. "I wouldn't hold your breath waiting for me to blindly follow your orders. I'm an experienced guide, Ronin, and I'm not stupid. I won't put myself at unnecessary risk, but if someone needs help, I won't stand by on the sidelines and do nothing."

He was a big, brooding presence at her back as she went upstairs to her guest room. She used the closet in there to store her cold-weather expedition gear.

She pulled it out and laid it on the bed. Ronin lounged in the doorway, dominating the small room.

"This house is a pretty big place for one," he noted.

"It's my dream home." She packed some things in her duffel bag. "I'm planning to grow into it, starting with getting my dog."

He grunted. "What kind?"

"A beagle." She looked at him and tilted her head. "Let me guess. You live in a loft apartment. No decorations, no photos, no food in the fridge, and a giant TV in the living room."

He shifted uneasily. "I'm a single guy."

She zipped the duffel closed. "Uh-huh. Not a closed-off man afraid to take emotional risks."

A scowl appeared on his face. "This—" he waved a hand at her house "—is not for me. There'll be no wife, no kids, and no picket fence in my life, Peri." His face closed down and he straightened. "You finished?"

She hefted the duffel bag. "Yes."

"Then let's go. We have a plane to catch to Antarctica."

---

RONIN SETTLED BACK in his seat on the plane. He knew right before a mission was the time to rest and conserve strength...because you never knew when everything was going to go to hell.

They were currently en route to Aurora Station. After an overnight flight to Santiago, Chile, followed by the smaller hop to Punta Arenas, they were all a little tired. They were currently sitting in the cargo area of the Ilyushin 76 that was their ride to Aurora. Darcy had managed to snag them all seats on a cargo plane already bound for Aurora.

He knew the Russian-made aircraft wasn't a military plane, but it had a similar feel. The long cargo area was currently packed with strapped-down pallets and several snowmobiles destined for research stations. The passenger seats ran along the walls with large, military-style seatbelts. As a SEAL, he'd spent too many hours to count on planes like this. Hell, as a CIA agent, he'd snagged a few flights home on military cargo transports, as well. He'd been on so many planes heading to so many different places, they all blended together.

Across from him, Logan and Dec were napping. Ronin glanced beside him at Peri. She looked relaxed but there were dark circles under her eyes. He'd watched her on the flight down to Chile, and she hadn't slept much. He guessed thoughts of her sister were keeping her from resting.

Like him, she was dressed for the trip. She wore heavy-duty cargo pants, and a few layers of tight, long-sleeved tops that clung to her toned upper body. The uppermost one was a dark green that looked striking with her hair, which was currently pulled up in a knot at the back of her head. It was clear she kept in shape with her climbing...and it was also clear she had perfectly-sized breasts—not too big, not too small.

He closed his eyes. *Dammit, Cooper, you aren't supposed to be noticing her breasts.* Except that since she'd blasted into his life, he had trouble not thinking of her. She was pretty and vibrant, and loved her sister. She also tasted so damn good.

That fiery, wild kiss they'd shared at the cabin kept tormenting him. Whenever he closed his eyes, the memory slammed into him. He wanted more.

*Still not supposed to be thinking of her.* He turned his

head and looked out of one of the few small circular windows. In the distance, the horizon was filled with a huge sheet of white. He was finally going to get the chance to visit the one continent he hadn't been to before.

"We're getting close," he said.

Peri unstrapped herself and pressed one knee to the seat to look out of the window. Her shoulder pressed against his, sending a tingle down his arm.

"The coldest, driest, and windiest place on Earth," she said.

"Ninety-eight percent of the place is covered in ice." He'd done his research. "And the ice averages almost two kilometers in thickness."

"I've visited McMurdo Station twice." She looked back at him. "The largest US station. But most of my trips have been to the Arctic. Amber has much more Antarctic experience than me." Peri dropped back into her seat, her hands clenching on her thighs.

Ronin stopped trying to talk himself out of touching her. He grabbed her hand. "This is her terrain. That puts her at an advantage."

Peri nodded. "Have you met this Dr. Browning at Aurora Station before?"

"Yes, Melinda is really salt of the Earth." He smiled. "What you see, is what you get. I like her. She doesn't lie and speaks bluntly."

"That must be refreshing for a former CIA agent."

"You can say that again."

She squeezed his fingers. "I don't lie either, Ronin."

He felt himself caught by those pretty blue eyes

again. Damn, what was it about this woman that tugged at him like this? "Peri—"

Her fingers tightened on his. "Just let yourself feel, Ronin." A faint smile on her lips. "I promise I won't hurt you."

Suddenly, Dec let out a yawn and leaned forward. "Where are we?"

Ronin let go of Peri's hand. "Just coming in over Antarctica now."

It wasn't long before the pilot's voice came over the speaker. "Prepare for landing. It can get a little bumpy."

"I do not love ice runways," Peri said.

"This aircraft was designed to land anywhere," Ronin reassured her. "It was designed for this."

They touched down smoothly, only bouncing a little, the engines roaring. Finally, they rolled to a stop.

He looked over at Peri. "Welcome to Antarctica."

PERI PULLED ON HER NAVY-BLUE, cold-weather jacket. It was rated for the extreme cold, and was waterproof and windproof. She pulled the faux-fur-lined hood up, and yanked on her very expensive, ultra-warm gloves. They were very thin compared to most styles, hence the price, but they were worth it for the extra dexterity. Once she'd grabbed her duffel bag, she walked down the cargo ramp of the plane behind the men.

They were all in their cold-weather gear as well, carrying their bags.

When the cold hit her, she stopped and let herself

adjust. The first punch was always shocking, exhilarating. She waited while the cold stole her breath away, like her chest was frozen, and then her lungs started working again.

She stepped out onto the snow. There was sunlight right now, but she knew it would only last a few more hours. The daylight hours were short this time of year, and very quickly getting shorter.

Several people started working, unloading the cargo for Aurora Station. Three people wearing bright-red jackets were waiting for them. It was hard to tell from a distance if they were male or female.

Not far behind them lay the research station itself. It was a motley grouping of buildings. All of them were up on stilts to keep them off the snow and ice. The largest one was rectangular, and she guessed it was the main living area. The rest were different sizes and shapes, one of them even a perfect sphere that made her think of a golf ball. She assumed some of these had to be research labs.

Dec strode ahead to meet the group. As they got closer, Peri focused on the person closest to them. The woman was smiling widely, and had a wrinkled, weathered face that was surrounded by wisps of gray hair that had escaped the hood of her jacket. A patch on the chest of her jacket said Aurora Station. On her arm was a patch of the Australian flag.

Beside her was a smaller woman, probably only a few years older than Peri, with dark eyes and hair. The patch on her arm was Chilean. The final member of the group was a tall, thin man, with pale skin and blue eyes. The scruff on his face was a pale, ginger color, so she guessed his hair was a similar color to her own. The flag on his arm was blue with a yellow cross. She had to think for a second, but she was pretty sure that was the flag of Sweden.

"It's colder than a polar bear's butt today," the older woman said in a husky voice with a heavy Australian accent. She waved toward the buildings. "Welcome to cold-ass Aurora Station."

"There aren't any polar bears in Antarctica, Mel," Dec said dryly.

"I know." She swiveled to lead them toward the station itself. "But a penguin's butt doesn't have the same ring to it. Let's save the introductions until we're inside."

They marched across the snow, and soon were moving up the stairs and into the rectangular building. Inside, they were met with a blast of heat.

"Thank fucking God," Logan grumbled under his breath.

The room was dominated by rows of tables, and there was a kitchen off to one side. Shelves lined the other side of the room, filled with books and board games, and there were a few comfy couches.

The older woman yanked her gloves off and pushed her hood back. She stripped off her coat, and hung it nearby. There were hooks on the wall, with several red jackets hanging from them. Peri saw that Dr. Browning's hair wasn't completely gray, but more salt-and-pepper, and pulled back in a bun.

As Ronin and Logan started taking off their jackets, Peri did the same.

"Nice to see you again, Declan." The woman engulfed the man in a hearty hug. "You're always a sight that's easy on the eyes."

Dec smiled. "And you never change, Mel."

She gave a cackling laugh. "Life's too short, my boy." Her gaze moved over to the others. "I see you brought me some more eye candy."

Logan snorted and the smallest smile touched Ronin's lips. For a second, Peri stared at his mouth. Since they'd left Denver, she felt the distance he was putting between them. Peri didn't like it.

"You remember Logan and Ronin," Dec said.

"Sure do. My mountain man and my G-Man." She hugged both the men.

Peri swallowed a smile as the THS members stoically accepted the woman's affection. G-Man. That nickname suited Ronin, with all his former CIA stealth.

"G-Man?" she said when he stepped back beside her.

"She's always called me that."

"Well, I think I might have to steal it."

"These are my two right-hand peeps, who help me keep Aurora running smoothly." Melinda nodded at the man and woman. "Dr. Gabriela Varela and Dr. Lars Ekberg."

"And this is Peri Butler," Ronin said. "She's an experienced polar guide."

"Nice to meet you, Peri," Melinda said.

"You, too." Peri shook the woman's hand. "Thanks for helping us."

"Now, I know you're keeping your mission a big fat secret from me." Melinda screwed up her nose. "And frankly, I probably don't want to know. We have two snowmobiles ready for you, and outfitted with everything you'll need."

"I'd like to bring you up to speed," Dec said. "You might be able to help us out. It just wasn't something I could discuss over the phone."

Mel nodded thoughtfully. "Okay. But I wouldn't want to be heading out this time of year."

"We'll be fine," Dec assured her.

"Well, there's a storm moving in. It's not expected to last long, but it looks nasty. You won't be able to leave today."

Peri felt a bolt of frustration and she barely managed to swallow a curse.

"But I have bunks for you and a hot meal." Then Melinda's face tensed. "And I have another problem to deal with. We have two researchers missing. They went out this morning to collect ice samples. They missed check-in and they haven't returned."

Peri's gut clenched. That was bad. The chances of survival out here if you hit a problem were slim.

"Lost a good researcher last year." Melinda's tone was charged with grief. "Fell in a crevasse. Hoping these two are still okay and just need a rescue."

Peri was well aware of how dangerous crevasses could be. The huge cracks in the ice could be deep, and could open up without notice.

She saw the THS men all straighten and share a look.

"They have any gear with them to survive the storm?" Dec asked.

"They have some basics," Gabriela responded. "A

tent, emergency blankets, and MREs. It wouldn't be comfortable, but they could survive. But not for long."

"We have search teams heading out now," Lars said.

"Let us help," Dec said.

Relief crossed Melinda's weathered face. "I'd appreciate it."

Lars stepped forward. "Everyone's going out in teams of two on snowmobiles. We have search areas mapped out based on their route and destination."

Dec looked at Logan. "You're with me."

Ronin turned to Peri. "Which means you're with me."

Peri nodded, glad to focus on something other than her worry for Amber. "Let's go." She grabbed her jacket. "But I'm driving."

Logan snorted and Ronin frowned. "No."

"You got to drive back in Denver, so now it's my turn, G-Man." She raised a brow. "Besides, I bet I have way more hours on a snowmobile than you."

Dec was grinning. "The lady has a point, Coop."

Grumbling, Ronin pulled on his jacket. "Fine."

# CHAPTER EIGHT

R onin watched Peri check the snowmobile. It was clear she had a lot of experience.

This machine was big and rugged, with skids at the front, and plenty of room for storage at the back. Finally, she climbed on, settling her hands on the controls. She looked back at him.

"Sure you can handle the back seat?" Her smile was pretty close to smug.

Ronin climbed on behind her and wrapped his arms around her. Even covered in her heavy-duty jacket, she felt incredibly small in the circle of his arms. As he crossed his gloved hands, he rested them over her belly, and he heard her breath hitch.

He made sure his mouth was close to her ear. "I'm pretty comfortable taking the rear."

She swiveled her head, her eyes on him. "I can't tell if you're making a suggestive remark or not."

He shot her a small smile. Damned if he didn't like

teasing her. Ronin had never teased anyone before. When he spent time with a woman, it involved a few drinks, followed by sex. There had never been teasing.

Peri shook her head. "You should smile more often, Ronin. It looks good on you."

He blinked at her, and realized he was smiling.

She turned on the engine and revved it, letting it warm up. A moment later, Dec and Logan pulled up beside them in a spray of snow. Logan was sitting on the back of the machine, holding the handles behind him.

"Ready?" Dec asked.

"Ready," Peri said.

Dec and Logan pulled ahead and Peri gunned it, following.

As they left Aurora behind, they split off from Dec and Logan. They had a search area slightly west of the others.

Ronin scanned their surroundings, taking in the landscape. Behind them was white as far as he could see. Ahead, the dark smudges of the Ellsworth Mountains tinted the horizon. Somewhere in there was the pyramid structure and Silk Road.

He tightened his hold on Peri. He hoped to hell that Amber Butler was still alive. Fucking Silk Road and their drive for money and power. They used whoever they wanted to use, and killed anyone who stood in their way. He sure as hell hoped Peri didn't have to cope with the loss of her twin.

He turned his head and spotted huge, dark-gray clouds lining the sky.

They did *not* want to get stuck in that storm front.

He looked down at the map and checked the GPS coordinates. He leaned forward. "We need to start there," he yelled over the roar of the engine. He reached past her and pointed. "We'll sweep back and forth."

She nodded, and she turned to follow his directions. As she moved the snowmobile into the search pattern, she handled the machine with obvious ease. They fell into the monotonous routine of zig-zagging back and forth, with no sign of the missing scientists, or their snowmobile.

All of a sudden, Peri cursed and yanked the snowmobile violently to the left. Ronin tightened his hold to stop from flying off.

She pointed and he saw the crevasse. The deep gash had opened up in the snow like someone had sliced it open with a knife. Peri turned the machine and they circled around the hazard.

They kept moving. Nothing. And the damn storm was getting close now. Ronin glanced at his watch and saw that it was check-in time. He pulled out the radio and tapped Peri's shoulder. She pulled to a stop.

"Aurora Station, this is Scout Three checking in."

"Acknowledged, Scout Three." Mel's deep voice came across the line. "Any luck?"

He heard the hope in the station leader's tone. "Nothing yet. Anything from the other teams?"

"Not yet."

"We have a bit more time before the storm will force us back. We'll keep looking."

"Thanks, Ronin. Stay safe."

Peri and Ronin continued on. He knew it was hard to

lose team members. He'd lost several over the years—a few fellow SEALs and a couple of CIA agents he'd worked with. None of their deaths had been pretty or easy, but they'd done their jobs. They'd believed in fighting to protect their country.

Ronin had joined the Navy to get an education, and because he'd known no one would grieve if he died in combat. Instead, he'd found a place to belong for the first time, and had brothers he'd cared about. But he'd always held himself apart. He didn't have the genes for the easy camaraderie so many had shared.

But he'd still felt their loss when they'd died.

His jaw clenched. He'd lost plenty of sleep over their deaths, and wondered what he could've done differently to help save them. Or, why it hadn't been him—with no wife, kids or family—who'd died.

"What's that?"

Peri's voice jerked him back. He peered ahead and spotted something dark on the snow.

She sped up and they hit a small bump, going airborne. They landed with a rattle, and it wasn't long before he could pick out the shape. Definitely a snowmobile.

"It has to be them!" Peri said.

They got closer, and worry skated across Ronin's nerves. He scanned the area around them. He didn't see anything that should trip his instincts, but something definitely felt wrong.

They pulled to a stop near the abandoned snowmobile.

Peri slid off. "Where are they?" She turned her head.

"Maybe they were working around here, and fell in a crevasse?"

"Maybe." They both circled the vehicle and Ronin slammed out an arm to stop Peri.

"Oh, God." She pressed a gloved hand to her mouth.

Ronin gritted his teeth. He slid his hand into the pocket of his jacket specifically designed to hold his Glock.

The two scientists were lying on the snow. One, a man, was flat on his back and staring sightlessly up to the sky.

The woman was on her side, blood coating the snow near her head. It was the same bright red as her jacket.

"Stay here." Ronin lifted his Glock and moved toward the bodies. He knelt between them and pulled his glove off. He loosened their jackets enough to check each one for a pulse.

"Fuck." He looked over his shoulder at Peri. "They're dead."

---

THIS HAD to be Silk Road.

Her belly churning, Peri pressed her hand to her mouth and looked away. She'd seen some bad injuries on her expeditions, but never anyone who'd died violently like this.

If Silk Road did this—killed two innocent people with no link to them, or knowledge of what they were doing—what would they do to Amber?

Peri forced herself to look back and watch as Ronin

checked the scientists over. Finally, he rose. "They were shot."

"God." She shook her head. Those poor people.

A muscle ticked in Ronin's jaw as he strode over to the snowmobile. He snatched up the radio and took a deep breath. "Scout Three to Aurora Station."

"Receiving, Scout Three, go ahead," Melinda responded.

"We found them."

An excited sound came through the line. "Are they okay? What happened—?"

"Sorry, Mel. They're both dead."

Silence on the line. Then Peri heard an expulsion of breath. "Acknowledged, Scout Three—" Melinda's voice broke.

Ronin kicked a boot at the snow. "Mel, they were shot. This wasn't an accident."

"Shot?" The station leader's voice was sharp with shock.

"Call all the other search teams in now. Whoever did this could still be out here, somewhere."

"Acknowledged. And Ronin...please bring them home."

"I will." He tucked the radio away, and turned to Peri. "I'll wrap the bodies and secure one on each snowmobile. Are you okay to drive back?"

She felt acid rising in her throat, but she swallowed it down. These people deserved to go home. "Yes."

As she watched him pull some tarpaulins and ropes out of the storage compartments on the snowmobiles, she felt cold and hollow. He took his time, wrapping the bodies and tying them onto the back of the vehicles. Peri helped where she could, feeling numb from her head to her toes.

When she was finally seated on the snowmobile again, she was very conscious of the woman's body behind her, but Peri locked her emotions down.

As she took off, following Ronin's snowmobile, she just focused on making it back to the station before the storm hit. Already, the light had turned to a murky gray, and the temperature was falling.

When they finally pulled into the station, she was cold, numb, and sad. The others were there to meet them. A stricken Lars stepped forward, with several other researchers, and they untied the bodies and took them away.

Melinda stood nearby, her face ravaged. Dec stood beside her.

"I'm so sorry, Mel," Ronin said.

She nodded. "Thanks for bringing them in from the cold." She cleared her throat and looked at Dec. "I'm guessing this could be related to the reason you're down here?"

Dec's face was grim. "It could be. You trust all your people?"

"I've worked with most of them for several seasons, but some are new." She blew out a breath. "Down here, we depend on each other. For our work, our safety, our emotional health. I want to say yes, I trust them all, but..." She stared off in the direction the bodies had been taken.

Peri reached out and grabbed Melinda's hand. "I

promise, if this is related to our mission, the person who did this will pay."

Melinda squeezed her hand. "Thank you." Then the station leader looked up. "Storm's here. We should get inside. You've all been assigned rooms, and dinner will be served in the dining room in an hour. Showers are limited to three minutes, but the water's hot." She tried for a smile. "You only get longer if you share."

Peri saw that Melinda was trying to lighten the mood, or distract herself from the terrible circumstances. "Where do you get your water?" She knew water supply was a crucial issue for research stations.

"We have year-round snow here," Melinda replied. "We have snow melters heated by solar panels and topped up by the generators. We store all the water in tanks in a heated tank house."

Peri knew that freshwater could be tricky for Arctic and Antarctic stations. If you had no easy source of water, like a melt lake or snow, you needed to drill for it.

As they headed inside and stripped off their gear, Peri moved on autopilot. Just putting one foot in front of the other felt like a huge effort. A cheery young woman told them all their cabin numbers, and waved them through to the sleeping quarters.

"Communal bathroom, I'm afraid," the woman said. "Far end of the hall. If any of you have the cabin next to Joe, I'll apologize now. Man snores louder than a freight train."

Dec slipped into his cabin. Then Logan. When Peri opened the door to hers, she took in the simple bunk with a dark-blue cover, built-in desk, drawers under the bed, and shelves above it. A small oval window showed nothing but gray beyond. Her duffel bag rested on the bed.

"See you for dinner," Ronin said behind her.

She couldn't meet his gaze, just nodded. She needed a hot shower, and some time to let everything sink in.

A hand gripped her shoulder. "You okay?"

"Just tired."

"Death is always hard," he said quietly.

She swallowed. "You've lost a lot of work mates."

"Yes. It never gets easier."

And when there was no one to hold you and help you feel alive, it had to be even harder. But right now, Peri knew if she held on to him, she'd break down. "See you at dinner." She closed the door between them.

Peri unzipped her bag, pulling out some clothes, but her vision blurred with tears. Damn, she hated crying. But now the hollow feeling burst open, and she was flooded with emotions. She couldn't stop thinking about those poor scientists. And worse, she was so deathly afraid for Amber.

*Tears never help, Peridot.* Her mother's voice. *But they can help purge the hurt.* Yeah, well, purging would have to wait.

Quickly, Peri grabbed her things, and headed for the showers at the end of the hall. The large room contained several stalls, and she stepped inside one, pulling the curtain closed behind her.

She stripped off and flicked on the water. She let the hot water beat over her face, and then the tears came. She just stood there, crying, sobs breaking free of her chest.

The water cut off, but the sobs didn't stop. God, she knew crying never helped and didn't solve a damn thing. But right now, she felt so alone. The ache inside her for her missing sister was huge.

A second later, hard arms wrapped around her from behind. She jolted, and then she smelled Ronin. He reached around her and flicked the shower on again.

She stared down at his muscular arms and the dark dusting of hair on them. Strong arms that could help hold her up for a little while.

She spun to face him. He was naked, and even harder and more ripped than she'd imagined. A jolt of something else shot through her. "Make me forget, Ronin. For a few minutes, I need to forget those bodies, Silk Road, the trouble my sister is in."

His lean face was serious. "Peri—"

She pressed her hands against his chest. He was so warm. "Come on, G-Man, just for a minute." She went up on her toes and kissed him.

His lips were firm, and at first, they didn't move. She nibbled at them, then scraped her teeth over his stubborn jaw.

"You going to call me G-Man now?" His hands flexed on her skin.

"It suits you." When she went back to kiss his cool lips, they parted. With a groan, he kissed her back.

*Oh, God.* His tongue thrust into her mouth and sensation flooded her. His kiss was forceful, firm, and so good. It forced her head back and the deeper he kissed her, the more she forgot. She pressed against him and just felt.

The water shut off again.

"Touch me." She heard the plea in her voice.

He lifted her arm and pressed a kiss to the inside of her wrist. He sighed. "You're vulnerable right now—"

She made an angry noise. "Upset, sad, afraid, and mad. But I know what I'm doing, Ronin. We both know that we've been attracted to each other from the first moment we saw each other."

He stared at her for a long moment, and then turned and snatched up their towels. He slung one around his hips and then, taking his time, he toweled her off.

Her heart felt like it was dancing in her chest. He took his time and then wrapped it around her. He scooped up their clothing in one hand, grabbed her hand with his other one, and pulled her out of the bathroom. A second later, he opened the door to his cabin, and tugged her inside.

Shut in the small space, she turned and looked at him, taking in his muscled chest, bronze skin, and the barely concealed bulge behind his towel.

Peri shivered, but it had nothing to do with the cold.

# CHAPTER NINE

He shouldn't touch her.

Ronin knew the moment he'd heard Peri crying in the shower that he should have turned and walked away.

But he couldn't ignore her or her pain.

As he stared at her now—her pretty face framed by wet hair—he knew he should walk away now, as well. "Peri—"

She moved, and lay back on his bed, letting go of her towel at the same time.

Every muscle in his body went rigid. She was so damn beautiful. All toned muscles and subtle curves.

"Touch me, Ronin." She cupped her breasts.

"So damn pretty, Peri." And strong. Her arms and legs were lean and trim.

She slid one hand down her belly, and then lower. She had a small patch of copper curls between her legs, and when she touched herself, she made a small noise in the back of her throat. His cock throbbed, and he watched with avid hunger. He knew he couldn't look away, even if the station was on fire.

She gasped, her lips parting, and she spread her legs a little. "Don't you want to touch me, Ronin?"

He growled. "Are you trying to seduce me?"

She made a choked sound. "Well, if I wait for you, we'll both be old and gray and still staring at each other when we think the other isn't looking."

Her fingers stroked between her folds and she moaned.

Ronin's control snapped.

He pressed a knee to the bed and leaned over her. He rarely took what he wanted. All his life, he'd forced down his own desires. But now, he lowered his head and slammed his mouth down on hers. The kiss was wild and hungry. Then, he trailed his mouth down her neck, across her collarbone, and over her breasts. He sucked one nipple into his mouth.

She arched up, her hands sliding into his hair. "Yes, right there."

He liked a woman who knew what she wanted. He licked and then blew on her nipple, watching it pucker even more. He slid his mouth across to her other breast. When she writhed beneath him, he slid downward, pressing kisses to her belly.

"Do you want my mouth on you, Peri?"

Her hips rolled. "Yes."

He moved lower. "You're so pretty here, too. And wet."

"Now!"

"When I say." He nipped at her thigh and loved her small cry. "I'm going to lick you, suck you, and make you come. Don't you dare hold anything back, Peri. I want it all."

Her breaths were coming in hard pants. "Okay."

He dragged a knuckle through her wet folds. "Gorgeous." Then he leaned forward and licked her.

She came up off the bed, but he held her down with his other hand. He delved his tongue inside her. Damn, she tasted so fucking good.

Her hands tugged hard at his hair. "I need you, Ronin. So bad."

He teased her swollen clit with the tip of his tongue, and slid a finger inside her. Her moan was long and loud. He kept teasing her, could spend all night right here. He slid a second finger inside her, and the need was a brutal, wild thing slamming through him with every beat of his heart. As he worked her, her moans turned ragged and impatient.

Her strong thighs wrapped around his head, and he moved to close his mouth on her clit. He licked once and then sucked.

Her hips rocked up, her heels sinking into his shoulders. Her orgasm hit her hard, and as a cry ripped out of her, he slid a hand up to her lips. She bit down on his palm to muffle her cries.

When Ronin raised his head, air sawing in and out of his lungs, she was lying in a boneless sprawl on his bed. *Damn*. Her eyes were glowing, her cheeks were flushed, and he'd never seen anything quite as tempting.

His cock was rock hard and throbbing painfully.

He was reaching for her again, when a knock pounded on the door. Ronin froze.

"Ready to eat, Coop?" Dec called out.

Peri giggled softly. "You already did."

Ronin pressed his palm over her mouth. "I'll meet you there."

She pressed a kiss to his palm.

"Roger that," Dec said, through the door.

*Great.* Dec had almost caught him naked with their client. Yes, Dec had married a former client, and half of THS had fallen in love on various missions, but it wasn't a line Ronin had ever crossed before. Hadn't ever been tempted to cross.

He felt Peri's hand graze his stomach and he caught it before it went lower. He dropped his forehead to hers. "This shouldn't have happened."

She stiffened. "Why?"

She expected him to have a rational conversation while she was lying naked beneath him? He rose off the bed and tightened the towel around his waist. "You've had a shock, and you're a client—"

"Oh, pfft." She stood, completely naked and unconcerned, with her hands on her hips. "You can lie to yourself all you want, Ronin. Yes, I've had a shock, and I'm a client. So what? Thank you for giving me something else —something really great, and pleasurable, and sexy—to think about. It was nice to feel good for the first time in weeks." She snatched up her towel and wrapped it around herself, tucking the end between her breasts, then she picked up her scattered clothing. "I'm going to get dressed. You can stay here and brood, and think up some better excuses as to why we shouldn't be naked together, in bed, with your cock inside me, while I'm gone." She winked at him, then looked down at his tented towel. "You can also dream of me returning the favor at a later date. I know I will be."

With that parting line, she slipped out the door.

Ronin dropped onto his bed with a groan. Her words echoed in his head, and a jumble of X-rated images formed. He closed his eyes. *Damn, woman.*

———

PERI TOSSED IN HER BUNK. She glanced at the glow of her watch on the bedside table and saw that she'd dozed for a few hours. But now she was wide awake in the middle of the night.

With a huff, she tossed the covers off and climbed out of bed. She needed the bathroom, and to curse a certain stubborn-ass man a few more times in her head. He'd practically ignored her at dinner and then disappeared.

She'd never worked this hard for a man before. If she wasn't convinced he was worth it...

Shaking her head, Peri hurried barefoot down the hall. Out of her room, the air felt quite chilly. In the bathroom, the lights were on very low, and she quickly used the toilet and then washed her hands in the small sink. She stared at her face in the small mirror. A face very similar to her sister's...

Suddenly, she saw a flash of movement in the mirror. She turned to see who'd entered the bathroom when white filled her vision.

Plastic fabric covered her face and then pulled tight at her neck. She coughed, bringing her hands up to tear at the fabric. Someone was choking her with one of the shower curtains.

Peri's attacker tugged her to the floor, pulling hard on the fabric. She tried to draw in a breath, but the plastic sucked up against her mouth. She couldn't breathe!

She started kicking and thrashing, and her attacker grunted. Whoever it was, they were strong. Peri twisted, trying to tug at the fabric.

It wasn't budging.

Her lungs started to burn and her vision wavered. *Fuck, no.* She wasn't dying here in Antarctica, and especially not before she'd rescued her sister. She rolled to the side, trying to break free. Her body rammed into something, and it fell over and crashed to the floor.

All of a sudden, the hard grip on the shower curtain was gone. Peri struggled to sit up, vaguely aware of slamming doors and shouts over the sawing of her breaths.

"Peri!"

Ronin skidded to his knees beside her, tearing the shower curtain off her. As his arms wrapped round her, she held onto him tight.

"What the hell happened?" Dec asked from the doorway.

Peri blinked. "Can I get some water please?"

A second later, Dec shoved a bottle at them and Peri chugged some water back.

"Peri?" Ronin brushed her hair back off her face. "What happened?"

"Someone attacked me. Tried to strangle me with the shower curtain."

Ronin went deathly still and she watched as his narrowed gaze went to the white plastic on the floor nearby. A scary look moved over his face.

"Ronin." Peri scrambled up on her knees, her hands digging into his arms. "You can't kill anyone."

"Yes, I can."

"Dec!" She looked up at him.

The other man nodded. "I've got it, Peri. Ronin, you take care of her, and Logan and I will track down the bastard who attacked her. You see him?"

Peri shook her head. "I saw white plastic and was kind of busy struggling to breathe. I don't even know if it was a man or a woman."

Ronin made a low growling sound and she pressed her face against his chest.

"What's happening?" Melinda's raised voice.

"Someone attacked Peri in the bathroom," Dec answered.

"What?" A disheveled Lars appeared right behind Melinda. "She must have slipped and fallen."

Peri shot the man a wry look. "Right. This is from a fall." She waved at her sore neck.

Ronin made another dangerous noise, his fingers brushing the angry red marks on her skin. He looked ready to kill someone. She became aware of everyone staring at them from the hall, voices arguing, and the icy coolness of the floor beneath her.

"Uh...G-Man, could you get me out of here?"

Ronin gave her a single nod and then Peri found

herself swept into his arms. Moments later, she was back in her room and he was setting her down on the bed. Feeling chilled, she pulled her knees up to her chest.

"Are you all right?" he asked.

She nodded. "I'm alive." She pressed her cheek to her knee. "Some asshole here must work for Silk Road."

"Yes. Dec will already be working with Mel to figure out who." A muscle ticked in Ronin's jaw. "It's standard Silk Road MO. They infiltrate everywhere and find vulnerable people who need money or are hungry for power."

And those were the people who had Amber.

Peri felt the walls of the small room closing in on her. She swallowed a few times, trying to calm herself. She was usually pretty unflappable, but this entire situation, and now the attack in the shower, had left her tense and edgy.

"Ronin?"

"Yes."

"I need some air."

His gaze sharpened on her. "It's freezing outside—"

She shot to her feet, trying to push her panic down. "I don't care."

He kept staring at her, then he nodded. "Get your gear on."

It only took Peri minutes to pull on her gear and boots. Soon, she and Ronin were pulling on their coats and hoods, and stepping out into the frigid night air.

Outside on the deck, Peri stumbled to a stop. "Oh, my God."

"That's damn impressive," Ronin said, awe in his voice. "The southern lights."

The storm had cleared and the entire night sky was painted an incredible palette of fuchsia pink, bright purples, and brilliant blues. Behind it, was the stunning display of the Milky Way.

"The aurora australis," Peri murmured. "I was here at the wrong time to see it last time."

They sat down on one of the steps, pressed together hip to hip and thigh to thigh. Once again, Peri found herself comforted by the solid presence of him. With his big body so close, she easily recalled how it felt to have his dark head between her legs, licking at her.

Desire curled in her belly and she felt a rush of dampness arrow between her thighs. She shifted a little.

Ronin slipped an arm across her shoulders. "Look up, Peri."

She did, captured by the magnificent view. She felt the tension drain out of her. "Tell me something no one else knows."

"A secret?" he asked.

"Anything."

"I picked the name Ronin when I was eight."

She turned to look at him now. He was still looking up at the sky. "Tell me."

"The hospital called me John, but once I entered the system, I was named Michael. Cooper was the surname of the first family I was placed with, but when I was eight, I learned about the ronin."

"It's Japanese, right?" she said.

ANNA HACKETT

He nodded. "My foster mother at the time told me I looked like I might have a little Japanese in me."

Peri studied his face, and guessed it was possible from his cheekbones and the shape of his eyes.

"A ronin was a samurai warrior without a master," he said. "A wanderer or drifter. The one I read about symbolized loyalty, sacrifice, and persistence."

Just like this man who was fascinating her more with every hour. "I think Ronin is the perfect name for you."

"It was something I took for myself, that no one could take away."

She leaned her head on his shoulder. "That's why I want a home. A place that's mine, filled with my things, and no one can take it away."

"And a beagle."

"Named Porthos."

"After one of the Musketeers?"

She nodded. "We were traveling through France when I was about ten. A lady in the village where we were staying had a beagle who'd had three pups. They were so cute and named Athos, Porthos and Aramis. Porthos climbed out of his basket and licked my face. It was love at first sight."

"I hope you get your Porthos one day, Peri."

"Right now, I'll settle for my sister."

His arm tightened. "Tomorrow. We'll find her."

Peri prayed he was right. "What do you think Silk Road is after?"

"Something dangerous. They're driven by money and power. But we took down one of their key people on our last mission, and something tells me whatever they're looking for will be something very dangerous. Something to help them shore up their power base."

She shivered.

"We need to get some more rest," he said. "We have a big day tomorrow."

Instantly, she felt her muscles tense. Going back inside didn't make her feel happy. "Ronin, will you stay with me?"

His arm tightened on her. "I'm sure as hell not leaving you alone again. You sleep and I'll make sure you're safe."

Warmth trickled through her chest. For the first time in her life, she knew in her bones that the person holding her wouldn't let her down.

# CHAPTER TEN

The next day dawned bright and sunny. Peri walked down the steps of the main building, and out onto the snow.

Ahead, three snowmobiles loaded with supplies, waited.

Lars was standing beside one vehicle, talking quietly with Declan, Logan, and Ronin. He was going to be their guide to the pyramid. Dec had apprised Melinda, Lars, and Gabriela of some of the situation with Silk Road, and the three station leaders had agreed to keep it quiet. They weren't happy about the fact that one of their own might be a traitor, but they didn't want anyone else to die.

Peri took a deep breath of crisp, clear air. She'd slept well for the rest of the night. After the attack, she'd thought she'd never get to sleep, but with Ronin's big body wrapped around her, she'd fallen asleep almost as soon as her head had touched her pillow.

She looked over at Ronin, drinking in his strong form.

Even in his bulky black jacket, he snagged her attention. Strength with a dark edge. In the past, she'd always gone for easygoing guys who enjoyed travel and adventure. Apparently dark, dangerous, and intense was her new type. *Not done with you yet, G-Man.*

As she approached, the men all called out to her, and she raised a gloved hand.

"Ready to head out?" Dec asked.

"Yes."

Lars nodded. "Excellent. The weather looks good, but things can change in a heartbeat. Best to get moving."

The men broke off to their snowmobiles.

Ronin looked down at her. "I'm driving today."

She inclined her head. "That sounds fair."

He climbed on the machine and she settled behind him. He started the engine, the vibrations going through her. Instantly, she thought of riding his bike with him. God, that felt like weeks ago.

She leaned forward. "Look at that. Here you are between my legs again."

His big body jolted and Peri smiled to herself.

"Behave," he growled.

She bit back a smile, and settled her goggles over her face. Moments later, they all pulled out, slicing across the snow. Lars was in the lead, followed by Dec and Logan, with Peri and Ronin bringing up the rear of their group.

The bright sun reflected off the snow and ice. Peri breathed deep. Everything looked so fresh, pristine, and untouched. Could there really be the ruins of an ancient civilization buried under the ice?

Soon, the mountains rose up ahead, dark rock poking up through the snow. The peaks all looked natural to her.

They skirted some rough ground, and kept moving.

A short while later, Lars pulled to a stop, and the other two snowmobiles flanked him.

"There," the scientist said, pointing.

Peri turned her head and sucked in a breath. Their goal sat at the end of a line of hills. A perfect pyramid of dark rock, spearing skyward through the snow.

They set off again, getting closer and closer. Peri kept her gaze trained on the rock. It was incredible, although she couldn't tell if nature had made it, or man. They zoomed past one side of the structure, and she scanned the surface. There were no signs of carvings or doorways, but the side looked very smooth and regular. It wasn't made of blocks of stone like the Egyptian pyramids.

Turning in a wide arc, they circled the pyramid. She noticed that Ronin was less interested in the pyramid, and kept studying the land around them, instead. She realized he was looking for any sign of Silk Road.

Finally, they all pulled to a stop.

"We'll take a look around on foot," Dec called out.

"Did you spot anything?" she asked Ronin.

He shook his head. "If they'd been here, there should be some sign. A camp, tracks, trash, something."

God, what if this wasn't Silk Road's destination? Peri's stomach turned hard, like a rock sat at the bottom of it. What if Amber wasn't here?

Lars, Dec, and Logan fanned out, beginning their manual search. Peri eagerly followed, keeping Ronin in sight.

Amber had to be here, somewhere. Peri trudged through the snow. She wouldn't stop until she found her sister.

But as she walked the line of the pyramid, she didn't see anything out of the ordinary. Her shoulders sagged.

There was nothing here but rock, ice, and snow.

---

AS THEY FANNED out around the structure, Ronin sensed Peri's growing tension.

They hadn't found any sign of Silk Road, or her sister.

He moved along the edge of the pyramid, stopping to look up the slick rock side. He still couldn't decide if it was manmade, or a natural formation.

Dec called out. Ronin waited for Peri, and together they hurried over to where Dec and Logan were standing, looking down at the snow. It had been flattened out, and possibly the site of a camp.

But there were no tracks.

"Could be a camp spot," Ronin said slowly.

"But nothing definitive," Dec said.

Peri kicked the snow. "There must be *some* sign that they were here."

They moved back around the next side of the pyramid. Lars was up ahead, looking at the snow.

"Anything?" Peri called out.

The scientist shook his head. "Doesn't look like anyone has been here."

Ronin glanced down where Lars' boots had left tracks

in the snow. He spotted a flash of color, partly buried, and strode over. As the scientist stepped back, Ronin knelt down and scratched away at the icy snow...and pulled out a red wrapper. He held it up.

Peri grabbed it and turned the wrapper over. Then she grinned. "It's a candy bar wrapper. They're Amber's favorite! She *always* takes a stash with her on trips."

Ronin looked around. "So, they were here."

"Where the hell did they go?" Logan asked with a scowl.

"There's nothing here," Lars said. "And this pyramid looks like a natural mountain to me."

Peri shook her head and turned in a slow circle, her gaze narrowed. Ronin watched her gaze zero in on a patch of snow nearby that looked churned up. She moved closer to it.

Suddenly, she let out a sharp cry, and dropped waist-deep into the snow.

"Peri!" He rushed toward her.

She was stuck in the snow, but she remained calm. "I'm okay."

Ronin grabbed her hand, worried she was dangling over the top of a deep crevasse.

"Careful," Dec called out.

"No, don't worry. I'm all right," Peri said. "My feet are touching firm ground." She scooped up the snow. "This is covering a shallow hole."

"Logan and Lars, get the foldable shovels off the snowmobiles," Dec ordered.

Ronin pulled Peri up and out, shocked that his heart

was hammering so hard. He watched her dust the snow off her clothes.

The men returned and soon started to shovel out the snow.

Finally, they all stepped back in silence.

"What the hell?" Peri breathed.

They'd uncovered an entrance to a tunnel, about seven feet in diameter.

"It goes down under the pyramid," Dec said.

Ronin crouched and craned his neck to look into the tunnel. It burrowed down into the ice below and was perfectly circular. "The ice looks like it's been melted to form this tunnel." What the hell had Silk Road used to make it?

"Can you see anything in there?" Peri asked.

Ronin pulled out a flashlight and shone it inside the tight space. The light glinted off something metal.

"There are five snowmobiles hidden in here."

"It's them." Peri crouched beside them. "We need to go in there."

"Let's grab our gear," Dec said.

They pulled their snowmobiles in close to the pyramid, and grabbed their backpacks. Each one was kitted out with tents, sleeping bags, rations, and other gear for surviving in the cold weather. Then, each of them clicked on their flashlights.

"We sure this is a good idea?" Lars said, his expression worried.

Ronin ignored the man, and dropped down into the tunnel. He reached up and caught Peri's waist as she climbed over the edge. He lowered her down, and the others followed them in.

They headed down the tunnel. The ground was slick and on a slight incline. They skirted the Silk Road snowmobiles, and Ronin heard Logan grumble. The big man's head was brushing the top of the tunnel.

Then, a moment later, the tunnel opened up into a large cavern.

"Wow." Peri shone her light upward.

The empty grotto was made entirely of white-blue ice. The slick walls looked like art.

"This is natural," Ronin said.

"Are we sure it's stable down here?" Lars asked.

"The ice is intact," Dec said. "No signs of cracking or instability."

They crossed the large space. Ahead, a giant wall of dark rock appeared out of the darkness. It was covered in places with a thin film of ice.

Then Peri stumbled to a stop. "Holy shit. Look at that."

Ronin moved his light to join hers. The two narrow beams illuminated a giant doorway in the rock. It was open, with darkness beyond.

*Fuck.* Ronin stared at it. The edges were ornate and lined with engravings.

"What the hell?" Dec said, staring at it.

Peri rushed forward, and pressed her gloved hand to the edge of the large doorframe. It was over twelve feet high.

"Look at this," she said, smoothing her hand down the rock. "There are inscriptions here."

Ronin moved his light and saw them more clearly now.

"They're similar to Egyptian hieroglyphs," Dec murmured. "Not quite the same. Some are different, and there are a few I've never seen before." He pulled out a small camera and took some shots.

"Let's go in." Peri stepped inside.

"We should think about this," Lars called out.

Ronin stayed right behind her. They moved quietly, and the only sound was their boots crunching on the ice.

The large tunnel was perfectly rectangular and lined with blue-ice walls. They glowed from within with a faint light.

"Where's that light coming from?" Logan's rumble echoed off the walls.

Ronin shrugged. "No idea. Some sort of phosphorescence?"

"Could be bioluminescence if there are organisms trapped in the ice," Dec added.

Ronin shook his head. This was all pretty incredible. The tunnel continued for a few more feet before a solid wall of ice stopped them.

Peri frowned. "That can't be it!"

"Maybe over the years, the ice has filled up whatever tunnels were down here," Ronin said.

"Over here," Lars called out.

The man was standing near a side wall a few feet back. He was shining his flashlight down toward the ground.

Another perfectly circular tunnel had been melted down into the ice. Ronin really wanted to see what tech

Silk Road was using to make their tunnels. He crouched at the edge, peering into the darkness. This tunnel was almost vertical.

The light didn't penetrate far. "No idea how deep it goes." Ronin caught Dec's gaze, and then Logan's.

"If it goes too deep," Dec said, "getting out will be hard."

"They had to have gone this way." Peri stabbed a finger at the tunnel. "My sister is down there, and running on borrowed time."

"You can't help her if you're dead," Dec said.

Peri pressed her lips together, and waited. Ronin hated seeing the helpless look on her face. He grabbed her hand. "We're going down."

Her gaze met his, a gleam in them. "Thank you."

Dec made a noise. "If we end up a mile under the ice, let's hope to hell Silk Road has a way to get out of there. Let's go...before my sense returns."

Ronin and Peri stepped up to the edge of the tunnel. He sat down on the lip. "This is going to be a hell of a slide. I'll go first."

"I'm coming with you." She moved in close beside him. "Ready?"

"Ready," he said.

He grabbed her hand and pushed off. They slid down the slick surface on their backs, gathering speed. The darkness swallowed them, and he kept a tight grip on Peri's hand and his flashlight. The beam of light danced dizzyingly on the tunnel's smooth surface.

They were moving fast, and he heard Peri make a

small squeak of unease. *Hell.* Ronin had no idea where they'd end up. He shoved the flashlight in his pocket and grabbed Peri. He hauled her closer until she was practically on top of him. She wrapped her legs and arms around him.

"Hold on!" he shouted.

They kept moving downward and soon it felt like they'd been sliding forever. Peri tightened her grip on Ronin's jacket.

"We're going deep. Really deep," she called out.

"I think the tunnel is flattening out." His voice echoed off the ice. "We're slowing down."

Without warning, they shot out of the tunnel and they were airborne. Ronin had the impression of pale light and ice. As they fell, he cursed loudly and Peri gripped him harder.

He twisted them midair. A second later, they slammed into the ground. He hit first, and Peri landed on top of him. Pain exploded through him and he groaned.

"God, are you okay?" She scrambled up, patting him down. "Anything broken?"

He sat up. "You aren't that heavy. I'm fine. You?"

She nodded. "You make a good landing pad." She grabbed her flashlight, turned, and shone it back at the tunnel they'd shot out of like some kind of damn waterslide. It was several feet off the ground. The echo of male voices filled the air and he knew the others weren't far behind.

Then she turned back and Ronin stood, dusting himself off. She looked beyond him and her jaw dropped.

"Oh, my fucking God."

He stiffened and spun, reaching for his gun. When he saw what she was looking at, he muttered, "Hell."

A perfectly intact rock temple rose up to fill the large cavern.

# CHAPTER ELEVEN

Peri's heart was a loud hammer in her ears. Like the previous cavern, the walls and ceiling of this one also glowed with a soft blue light and let her see the temple in all its glory.

It was carved from dark rock, with columns rising up in an elegant style vaguely reminiscent of Egyptian temples. The central part of the temple was pyramid-shaped, with neat rows of columns flowing away from it. A large opening at the front of the pyramid had apparently once had a waterfall flowing out of it, but it was now frozen solid in a drape of blue ice.

All of a sudden, a shout sounded behind them. Peri twisted, and saw a big body fly out of the tunnel. Logan hit the ground beside them with a solid thud. Cursing steadily, he turned and pushed to his feet.

A moment later, Lars and Dec landed. Lars lay sprawled on the ground, stunned, while Dec rolled athletically to his feet.

"Everyone okay?" Ronin asked.

"I think so," Lars said, rubbing his hip.

Dec nodded and hitched his backpack up higher on his shoulders.

Then Lars' mouth dropped open in shock. "My God."

Dec eyed the temple with no surprise, and Logan just put his hands on his hips and scowled. Peri figured they were both a bit jaded when it came to discovering fantastic lost temples.

"Well, Zach and Layne will be happy," Dec said. He lifted his camera.

"I can hardly believe this," Peri said. "It's true. There was a civilization here in Antarctica, once upon a time."

"Come on." Ronin grabbed Peri's hand and pulled her toward the structure.

They walked up some steps, and entered the temple complex proper. They fanned out, weaving slowly through the columns. Peri spotted more hieroglyphs etched into the rock. The columns looked more delicate than what she'd seen in Egypt, a little more refined and elegant. In places, ice covered the rock in a shiny blue film.

The central pyramid loomed ahead.

Dec looked up. "This might be directly beneath the pyramid above."

"Over here," Logan called out.

Anticipation shot through Peri, and she hurried over with the others. Logan was standing beside the remnants of a camp.

Peri bit her lip. There was gear stored by a rock wall

—backpacks, large water bottles, tents. She searched for any sign of Amber's gear, but nothing looked familiar.

"What the hell is that?" Logan toed a large piece of equipment that looked vaguely like missile launcher.

Ronin crouched. "Some sort of tech for making the tunnels. Could be a laser of some sort, I'm not sure."

"No time to examine it now," Dec said.

Ronin started opening the bags. He pulled items out, studied them, then discarded them. He pulled out a tablet in a heavy-duty case and tapped the screen. "It's password protected."

"Can you get into it?" Dec asked.

"Not as quickly as Darcy would." Ronin stood. "But give me a minute."

Peri watched as he expertly tapped commands into the tablet, and a second later, data filled the small screen.

He scanned it, before tilting it toward Dec. The other man cursed.

"What?" she asked. "What is it?"

"We know what Silk Road is after down here," Ronin said, his tone dark.

A shiver skated through her. *The weapon.* "How could they know what they were going to find down here?"

"They found a secret Nazi record." Dec shoved a hand through his hair. "The Nazis discovered this place when they were scouting to build a base here during the war."

Ronin lifted his head from the text he was reading. "And then Silk Road sent a recon team. They explored what they could, and recorded what they saw. Looks like their people managed to decode some of the hiero-glyphs." He showed her the image on the tablet.

It showed a metallic artifact. It was a small club with what looked like claws at either end. She'd never seen anything like it. The closest thing she could compare it to was a scepter that a king or queen would hold. "What is it?"

"It's called a vajra," Dec said.

"Which is what, exactly?" Peri asked.

Dec sucked in a breath. "Vajra is the Sanskrit word meaning both thunderbolt and diamond."

She blinked. "Sanskrit? It's Indian?"

Dec nodded. "It was a weapon that belonged to Indra, the god of rain and thunder. The vajra had the indestructibility of diamond, and the unstoppable force of lightning."

"It's a weapon," she said quietly.

"Yes," Ronin said. "This is what Silk Road is after."

"Goddammit." Dec pressed a hand to the back of his head. "I was hoping they wouldn't find anything here. If this is some sort of advanced tech, it could be really dangerous."

"We have to stop them," Ronin said.

"Yeah," Dec agreed.

*God.* Once again, Peri fought back a wave of intense fear for her sister. Silk Road had gone from antiquities thieves to possible terrorists after a deadly weapon.

"Let's keep moving." Dec moved up the main steps and through the pyramid's ice-coated entrance.

Inside the main pyramid, a blue-white light glowed.

"This place is incredible." Awe soaked Lars' voice.

"My guess is that some survivors from this civilization made it out and spread across the world," Dec said. "Some went to India, to South America, to North America, to Egypt. Layne loves to talk about the Egyptian legends of the Shemshu Hor. They were said to be survivors, wise mages, who settled in Egypt and shared their knowledge."

"Read about Viracocha," Logan said. "Creator god of the Inca. He wandered the world, sharing his knowledge of civilization." The big man lifted his head. "He was usually shown holding two thunderbolts in his hands."

Peri shook her head, trying to imagine bedraggled survivors of a catastrophe spreading out across the world to make a new life for themselves. She walked through the temple, and stared at the carvings on the wall. She could see things that looked Egyptian, Indian, and perhaps Incan as well. She stopped and pressed her hand to ice that had covered the image of a woman standing side-on, arms outstretched.

What had life been like here, in this lost civilization? What had it felt like when their world had tumbled and been destroyed? So many would have died, parents losing children, wives losing husbands, sisters losing sisters.

As they passed a giant slab of dark rock that had to be some sort of altar, Peri half expected to see priests and priestesses walk out with offerings to the gods. Another huge doorway leading out of the ice-covered temple appeared ahead.

She followed Ronin through the opening. They all paused and gasped. Finally, she saw something that also shocked Declan, Logan, and Ronin.

A small city lay spread out ahead of them.

In places, the buildings were pristine, like they'd just been abandoned moments before. In other places, the ice had crept in like a slow-moving wave, covering the structures.

"Look." Peri spotted some fabric lying on the ground at the bottom of the steps. She hurried down and snatched it up. It was a green wooly hat.

Peri clutched it to her chest and closed her eyes. "It's Amber's."

Her clever, brave sister was trying to leave clues.

"We need to keep moving." Ronin gripped Peri's arm and squeezed. "We might be able to catch up with them."

Dec nodded. "But at some point, we'll need to stop and rest."

Peri wanted to argue. She wanted to charge into this eerie, dead city and find her sister. But she was an experienced guide, and she knew better than to push too hard. It could cost them all their lives.

Ronin gripped her hand. "We can make it a bit farther before we take a break."

She smiled at him. It appeared he could read her like an open book, and she didn't care. Sometime during the last few days, Ronin Cooper had earned her trust. She followed him into the ancient city.

---

RONIN'S STEPS echoed dully off the ice-covered stone. They were walking down a street lined with what had probably been shops and homes. They crossed an open square, maybe once a park where children had played, but now just a slick, ice-covered space.

It must have been an amazing metropolis.

He glanced at the ground, noting the scuff marks of boots on ice. "They went this way."

Silk Road had left a clear trail for them to follow. The thieves clearly weren't expecting company.

The street turned, and ahead was a giant wall of ice in a cloudy blue-green. The street continued right alongside it.

Suddenly, Peri jumped back from the ice wall. "What the hell?"

Ronin spun, reaching for his Glock. "What?" He didn't see anything but ice.

She frowned. "I saw something move. *In* the ice."

Ronin looked at Dec, who shook his head. Ronin studied the ice wall again.

Then, there was sudden movement behind the ice, and his eyes widened. A huge animal swam past. It had distinctive black-and-white markings.

"Orca," he breathed. "There's water behind this wall."

"My God," Peri said.

Another large predator swam past with graceful moves. Ronin peered through the ice and spotted distorted shadows on the other side. Something else was out there.

"Dec? What do you make of that?" Ronin pointed. Something was definitely sitting on the other side of the ice in the cold water.

"They almost look like...vehicles," Dec said, a frown in his voice.

"Or submarines, maybe?" Peri added.

Dec took a few pictures. "They look ancient. My guess is they were made by the people who lived here. Layne is going to be *so* pissed she isn't on this mission."

They moved on. They passed through several more neatly-laid-out streets, following the boot tracks. Silk Road was moving deeper into the heart of the city.

"Look at that," Peri breathed.

Not far away, ice had infiltrated the city, creating a giant curve of ice that formed a cavern. She hurried over and glanced inside.

To Ronin, it looked like water had rushed in like a wave, and frozen. It was a beautiful blue-green color.

"The ground is rough in there," she said. "But the walls are smooth and gorgeous. It's amazing."

"Look at that." Ronin shone his flashlight upward.

Dec hissed in a breath. "That doesn't look stable."

The ceiling of the ice cavern was covered in sharp icicles.

"Well, I'm glad Silk Road didn't go that way," Logan said.

His voice echoed through the cavern, and a second later, several icicles crashed down to the ground like missiles.

They all leaped back.

"Shit," Peri muttered.

"Come on," Dec said. "Let's keep going."

They turned away from the ice cavern and headed back down the street. Soon, their group stepped out into a large main square. Ronin took a second to scan ahead, but didn't see any movement, or hear any sounds. A giant, rectangular stone dominated the square, set upright. It was covered in engravings.

They paused in front of it, and Dec moved closer, pressing a hand to the symbols. "Definitely similar to Egyptian hieroglyphs."

"Can you read it?" Peri asked.

"A little. When you grow up with a history professor and a treasure hunter for parents, you absorb a lot."

"And when you marry an archeologist who specializes in Egyptian history," Logan added.

Dec grinned. "I have better things to do with my wife than decipher hieroglyphs."

Logan snorted.

When Dec turned back to the stone, Ronin watched the man's brow crease. Dec let out a breath. "It talks about a terrible calamity, and the fall of the city. The ground shook and moved, and in days, the ice came and many died."

Peri pressed a hand to her mouth. "There would have been thousands of people living here."

"And very few survivors," Dec said. He looked back at the stone. "This stone is a remembrance and a warning."

"A warning?" Lars said.

"From what I can make out, it says greedy people used a great power, and that was what caused the destruction of the city."

Ronin cursed. "They used the vajra and it did this? Shifted an entire continent?"

"It says the city is the tomb of the great power, and that it shouldn't be tampered with. Any who enter here will find nothing but death."

Peri gasped. Ronin scanned the empty city.

"Where are the bodies?" he said.

"What?" Peri looked up at him.

"A catastrophic event froze the city fast, and only a few survivors made it out. Where are the bodies? You'd expect to see some frozen in the ice."

Dec frowned thoughtfully. "No idea. That's probably not a good sign."

Logan crouched nearby, studying the ground. He looked up at them. "Looks like the Silk Road group split up here."

Ronin studied the markings on the ice and nodded. "Half the group went that way—" he pointed down another street "—and the other half in that direction."

He pointed into what looked like a huge building that was mostly covered in ice.

"Why would they split up?" Lars asked.

"Maybe they could translate the entire stone," Dec mused. "It might give more information than I can read."

"Any way to tell which way Peri's sister went?" Logan asked.

Peri scanned the ground. "I don't see anything she might have dropped as a clue." She huffed out a breath.

Dec was silent for a moment. "We need to split up. Ronin and Peri, you head into the building. Logan, Lars, and I will go the other way. Ninety minutes, then we come back and meet here. Got it?"

They all nodded, everyone checking their watches.

Moments later, Ronin and Peri walked into the large building. His flashlight illuminated the vast, empty space.

"Their version of a warehouse?" Peri suggested, stepping cautiously on the floor. Here, the ice floor was bumpy and rough.

"Probably." Ronin picked his way through the space.

He tried to imagine what this place must have looked like in its heyday, bustling with people and life. He couldn't picture it.

They followed the Silk Road trail, moving through several other warehouses, all huge cavernous spaces. The next one had several rooms off the side, and Ronin felt the temperature rise a few degrees. Those rooms were free of ice, but empty of anything else.

"How are these rooms free of ice?" Peri asked.

Ronin crouched and pressed a palm to the stone floor. "It must be some sort of heated storage. Whatever is powering it must still be working."

"Amazing," she murmured.

The Silk Road trail led to the back of the warehouse... right up to where it stopped at a huge hunk of ice.

"What is this?" Peri said.

Ronin studied it and looked up. He cursed. "A huge chunk of ice broke off the ceiling and is blocking the doorway."

"Dammit," she said, swinging her light around. "Look, there's another doorway over there."

They headed in that direction. One of Ronin's boots slipped and he caught himself. "Watch yourself. The ground's slick here."

She nodded, moving slowly.

Then Ronin heard a loud crack.

They both froze. He looked down and saw a spider web of cracks in the ice beneath him. He frowned.

Then, the ground gave way, and he was falling.

A second later, he splashed into freezing-cold water. *Fuck.*

"Hold on, Ronin!" Peri shouted from above.

Ronin gasped, his breaths coming in fast pants. The water was freezing. He knew hyperventilation was the body's natural response to the shock of the intense cold, so instead, he focused on trying to control his breathing.

He tilted his head and looked up. He'd fallen down a cylindrical hole. It must have once been some sort of water tank or storage. His teeth clattered together, and his heart thumped hard in his chest. It was fucking cold. He pressed a hand to the ice wall. It was slick, with no handholds or cracks, or anything to hold on to.

He glanced upward again, watching as Peri climbed over the edge of the hole. She was lowering herself over the side, rigged to a rope. She moved with strong, experienced moves down the icy wall.

He blinked and smiled to himself. He had to admit he really liked her. Everything about her. She was strong, smart, and stubborn. She loved her sister and could curse like a soldier. It had been such a long time since he'd really liked a woman.

When she reached him, stopping just above the water, she was grim faced. "Take it easy. Contrary to popular belief, hypothermia takes a lot longer to set in than people think."

"I...know." His muscles were feeling sluggish, his

energy rapidly draining away. "Been plunged in...lots of freezing lakes...as a SEAL."

She reached down and held out an arm. "We need to get you out of there. Our muscles and nerves don't work well in the extreme cold."

Meaning he'd lose control of his muscles, and wouldn't be able to keep his head above the water. He tried to grab her hand, but his aim was way off, and he missed. His muscles were beginning to ache, badly.

"Come on, G-Man. Stay with me."

He tried again, and they connected. She pulled him closer, and he felt her lean down and wrap a rope around him. She tied it off with some impressive knots. Damn, he was so cold. He just wanted to close his eyes and make the pain go away.

"No, Ronin," she snapped. "Look at me. Stay with me."

He stared into her blue eyes, and kept staring. "Could...look at you all day."

She smiled. "Right back at you, G-Man."

They started upward. Ronin did what he could to help, but it was a hellishly tough climb. He heard each one of Peri's grunts and harsh expulsions of breath. They slipped a few times, smacking against the ice wall.

He saw the strain on Peri's face. She was killing herself to get him out. He frowned. That was unacceptable.

"Let me go," he mumbled wearily.

"Hell, no!" Anger fired in her eyes.

"No one's ever wanted me." He tried to stop the

words, but they tumbled out, slurred and broken. "Not even my mother. She tossed me away at birth."

"*I* want you. And I am fucking getting you out of here."

They kept moving, inching upward slowly. Just when he felt like his body had nothing left in it to give, Peri clambered over the edge. She yanked on the rope, and pulled him over.

He collapsed on the icy floor. He couldn't feel anything anymore.

## CHAPTER TWELVE

R onin wasn't moving and wasn't shivering. *Not good.* Peri's heart was lodged in her throat. Hypothermia was setting in, and she had to get him warm.

She slid an arm around him. "Come on, G-Man. Up we go."

She heaved, and he staggered to his feet. She gritted her teeth as she took his weight. God, he was heavy, and her muscles already felt like noodles after the climb out of the hole.

"Move nice and slowly," she warned him. "That heart of yours is working overtime right now." They shuffled across the ancient warehouse.

She led him into one of the ice-free rooms, and gently lowered him to the floor. She needed him horizontal to help the blood flow through his cold-constricted arteries. She ripped his backpack off, thanking whatever god might be listening that it was made of a high-tech waterproof fabric. She opened it and checked that everything inside was still dry. She opened her own pack too, grabbing what she needed. She quickly set up their two-man tent, and laid out their sleeping bags inside, zipping them together. Then she started tearing at his wet clothes.

"Time to get these off." Peri worked to get his clothes off, and then helped him onto the nest of sleeping bags. His eyes had closed, and he still wasn't shivering. She grabbed some small warming packs and cracked them to start the chemical reaction to heat them. She stuck them under his armpits.

Next, she wrung out his inner layers and hung them inside the tent. She set his boots inside as well, although they'd take much longer to dry. Hers and Ronin's bodies would be the heat source to dry everything off.

But first, she had to get him warm.

Hurrying, she stood and opened her jacket. She tossed it aside, and then stripped off her clothes including her silky, thin, thermal underwear. She tossed them in a pile inside the tent. Naked, except for her panties, the cold made her shiver.

She climbed into the tent, zipped it closed behind her. Then she wrapped herself around Ronin and pulled the sleeping bags closed, cocooning them inside.

With all the exertion, and the sleeping bags, she felt hot, but Ronin's skin was so icy cold against hers. She gritted her teeth, pressed into him, and shoved her face against his neck.

A faint moan rumbled through him.

"I know, babe," she murmured. "Come on, wake up and talk to me." *Be okay. Please.* She started stroking him.

His arms, his face, his strong jaw. She kept murmuring comforting nonsense to him.

It felt like forever, but finally, she thought his skin felt warmer. Then he started shivering.

Huge shivers wracked him, so hard his teeth were rattling. She held on to him. "I've got you, G-Man."

He groaned and moved fitfully.

"I'm here. Open your eyes, Ronin. Let me see those midnight eyes of yours." She kept talking, holding him tight as the violent shivers continued. She told him all about being a twin, her travels, why she liked climbing, how sometimes you could be surrounded by so many people and still feel alone.

Before long, she was covered in a sheen of perspiration, and his body was pumping off heat. Finally, the shivers subsided. She pressed a kiss to his bare shoulder. She was so damn glad he was going to be all right. When he'd fallen into the water, she'd been terrified.

His breathing evened out and she guessed he was asleep. He'd need some calories once he woke up. But for now, exhausted herself, Peri let herself doze, as well.

She wasn't sure how much time had passed, but she woke up to a hand sliding down the side of her body. She opened her eyes and took a second to orient herself. She smelled Ronin, and felt toasty warm.

Suddenly, she was rolled over, and his big body moved over hers. He pinned her down, shoving her legs apart.

She gasped and felt a very hard cock brush over the hot, damp center of her. She moaned, her fingers digging into his skin. She looked up into glittering, dark-blue eyes.

The heat and hunger she saw made her chest tighten.

"Ronin, you were just hypothermic. You need to rest—"

He reached down, his hand cupping her breast for a second, before he moved lower. He shoved aside her panties, and one thick finger speared inside her.

*God.* She'd gone from dozing to a barrage of arousal in seconds. She undulated her hips against his hand.

"Need you." His voice was deep and guttural.

She wasn't even sure he was fully awake. He seemed to be operating on instinct. And right now, his body was telling him he was very much alive, when not long ago, he'd been dangerously close to death.

His thumb brushed her clit, and Peri tried to stifle her cry. She stared up at the tough, intense man above her.

*Hers.* The thought reverberated through her. Nothing and no one had ever just been hers before. Something she could keep and be sure it would stay a part of her life. She sank her hands into his hair and yanked his head down. The kiss was hard, edgy, with the hint of teeth, and the deep drive of tongues.

The taste of him flooded her, and his tongue slid into her mouth, hard and demanding.

"Never tasted anything as good as you." He nipped her jawline, then found a sensitive spot on her neck that made her squirm.

With a jerk of his wrist, he tore her panties off.

She arched into him and felt the head of his cock

prod between her legs. Then, with one hard thrust, he drove inside her.

Peri moaned. It was fast, and there was nothing gentle about him. Sensation burned across her nerve endings. She felt very stretched and very full and she loved it.

He dragged out of her and then thrust back in with a flex of his hips. He pinned her down and started hammering into her with brutal thrusts. This wasn't gentle lovemaking, this was a hard, fast affirmation of life. She wrapped her arms and legs around him, and dug her nails into his tight ass, urging him on.

Each grind of his hips put pressure on her clit and she felt her release rushing at her. She'd never experienced anything like this—so primal, so raw. His big body covered her, filled her, and she loved it. She felt claimed and branded.

With every thrust, she heard a harsh expulsion of air from Ronin. He was thrusting into her with an urgency that made her body white-hot.

Her release erupted through her body. Her inner muscles clamped down on Ronin's cock and she came hard, sinking her teeth into his arm to muffle her scream.

---

RONIN FELT all of Peri's orgasm. Her sweet body gripped his cock, her muffled screams played in his ears, and he felt the sharp nip of her teeth on his skin. It was sexy as hell.

He ground his teeth together, his jaw tight. He

wanted to feel her come again. He used every ounce of his control to stop from slamming into her and emptying himself inside her.

He wanted to make sure she remembered this. That she remembered exactly how he made her feel, and how she felt with him inside her for the first time.

They could have both died out there in the freezing cold, and right now, the driving need inside him was to claim this woman.

He pulled out of her and she made a protesting noise, grabbing for him.

"Up." He urged her to her feet and turned her. The tent wasn't very big, and she was forced to bend over. He had the perfect view of her round ass, and the pretty sight of her just-fucked folds. He groaned and ran his fingers between her legs.

"What are you—" she moaned, pushing back against him.

"So fucking pretty, Peri." He stroked her, listening to her mewling cry. "Can't believe my cock fits in here. Did it stretch you out? Did it feel good?"

"Yes." A husky growl.

"I'm going to slide back in here and make you come again."

She jerked against his hand. Ronin sank back, resting on his knees, his throbbing cock hard as steel. "Yeah, you want that, don't you?"

"Yes. Yes."

He gripped her hips. "Sit back on my lap."

He helped her sink down slowly. He fisted his cock with one hand, and when her damp, slick flesh touched his cock, they both groaned. Every muscle in his body went tight. *Hold on. Don't come yet.*

"That's it, Peri. Sit on my cock. Take it all inside you."

She moaned and he controlled her movement, slowly sliding inside her warmth. It was torture.

Perspiration broke out on his skin until finally, she was flush in his lap, his cock lodged deep inside her. He nuzzled her neck and saw the curve of her flushed cheek.

"I'm alive because of you." He bumped his hips up and she moaned. "My hard cock is inside you, because of you."

"Please, Ronin...move." She wiggled her ass against him.

He clamped his hand on her hip and held her down. He slid his other hand up to cup her breast and tease her hard nipple.

She moved against him, moaning helplessly. "Move, damn you."

He smiled. His sexy woman wasn't the most patient when she wanted something. "Okay." He gripped both her hips, and used his strength to lift her, then slam her back down on his cock.

Her head flew back, hitting his shoulder. He worked her up and down his cock.

"Yes." She moved as well, helping him, her body rippling on his.

"Touch yourself," he whispered. "Reach between those sexy thighs and find that swollen clit."

She slid her hand down, and when she moaned, he knew she was close.

And fuck, he was riding the hard edge of the orgasm of his life. She rocked against him.

"That's it, Peri," he murmured. "Give me your mouth, baby."

She turned her head and he kissed her. As she came, her body shook, spasming around his cock. He swallowed her scream with his mouth.

Then he jerked her up and down another few times, and a blinding orgasm crashed into him. He roared his release, shooting deep inside her. It was strong enough that his vision actually dimmed for a moment.

Peri had slumped against him, limp and warm. He lowered them down onto the sleeping bags, their slick skin sticking them together.

*Christ.* Ronin pulled in a few deep breaths, running his hand through her hair. He'd had sex plenty of times. But this...this was something else.

He held her tight and listened to her harsh breathing slow down and even out. This was the bit he wasn't good with. He wasn't a snuggler, or someone to talk about his feelings. When he had sex, he ensured the woman enjoyed herself, and then he left.

Peri turned, wrapping her arms around him, and snuggled into his chest. Ronin relaxed. Apparently, Peri knew what to do.

She looked up at him from under mussed bangs. "Hey."

"Hey," he responded.

"You're okay?" She reached up and cupped his cheek, gently scratching a nail through his stubble.

"Thanks to you."

She smiled. "I think you paid me back with interest."

"I think I sort of...took you by surprise."

"For a second." She scratched his cheek again. "Don't think I wasn't an enthusiastic, willing participant."

*Shit.* "Peri, I didn't even think about protection—"

"It's okay. I'm on birth control and I got a clean bill of health at my last checkup."

Ronin blew out a breath. He'd never not used protection with a woman. "I'm healthy, too."

"Good."

He tightened his hold on her, a feeling of rightness moving through him. "I may never be able to let you go."

She leaned up and pressed a light kiss to his lips. "So don't."

Ronin felt parts of him that had never seen the light straining to get closer to her. "Peri—"

"I know. You're dark, bad, and dangerous." She cupped his cheek. "What happened to you, Ronin, to make you think you don't deserve some happiness?"

God, she cracked him wide open. "It wasn't one big, terrible thing. Just lots of smaller ones. From being an abandoned, drug-addicted baby tossed out like trash—"

"Which has nothing to do with you," she said fiercely.

He smiled sadly. "I watched so many people die while I was a SEAL. There were so many people I couldn't save. I watched good men and women lose limbs, their eyesight, or go home in boxes." He pulled in a shuddering breath. "I thought working for the CIA would help me find the missing chunks of my soul."

"And instead, it took more."

He nodded. "My last assignment was to help take

down a human trafficking ring." He closed his eyes, unwilling to sully what he'd just shared with Peri. "I saw women, hell, young girls, used and abused." God, the things he'd seen. His hand clenched in her hair. He breathed in the fresh scent of her. "I had to watch terrible things, and pretend I liked them, to get close to the people we needed to bring down."

She squeezed him tighter. "You did your part. You're one of the good guys, Ronin. A hero. And now, you deserve a life."

Ronin wanted to believe her. He cleared his throat. "How long was I out?"

"Half an hour." She glanced at her heavy-duty watch. "We've been gone about two hours."

God, it felt like a lifetime. Dec would have realized something had gone wrong by now. "They'll be looking for us."

"You need to eat something—" she sat up "—and drink something to get your strength back."

"Thought I just proved my strength was fine."

She rolled her eyes at him and reached over to the backpacks. As she pulled out some ready-to-eat meal packs, Ronin watched the sway of her pretty breasts.

She turned back, and handed him a package of food and a drink bottle. Then she realized he was looking at her. She glanced down, her cheeks going pink, then glanced back up at him, heat flickering in her eyes.

"You need to conserve some energy, Ronin. Not spend more of it."

"I want you again." He blew out a breath. "But there's no time." Hell, there hadn't been time the first time he'd had her, but he'd already been inside her before any conscious thought had moved through his head.

She leaned in and kissed him. He pulled her closer, and drank from her mouth.

"Later," she murmured. "After we finish this."

"Later," he promised. "Later, I want to fuck you from behind, and then wrap my hand in that pretty hair of yours while you suck my cock."

She raised a brow. "And I want your clever tongue between my legs again, and then I want to climb you and ride you hard."

His cock jerked. "You have yourself a deal, Peri."

---

PERI SPOONED some of the bland food into her mouth, chewing slowly. "We need to find Dec and the others."

Ronin was sorting through his clothes. She could see that the outer layers were still damp, but the inner layers that would be closest to his body were dry. Luckily, he also had dry socks in his backpack.

He pulled his thermal underwear on with a frown. "They should have come looking for us by now. I don't think we'd be that hard to find."

Peri finished eating. "They're probably close." Her body was still tingling, and she kept sneaking glances at Ronin as he dressed.

*God*, that body. He pulled his trousers on and she stifled a sigh. She'd been thoroughly fucked and possessed by Ronin Cooper. She quivered and felt a throb between her legs, a very physical reminder. She really wanted to do it again. And again.

She started pulling her own clothes on. But that would have to wait. Right now, she had a sister to save.

Soon, they stepped out of the tent. She zipped up her coat, and they quickly took down the tent and packed up the rest of their gear.

Strong arms yanked her close. As soon as his lips touched hers, warmth curled through her. Yep, she couldn't get enough of this man.

"Thanks again for the rescue," he said quietly.

"Anytime, G-Man."

His fingers brushed at her hair. "And thanks for the rest, as well."

"Anytime to that, too," she whispered.

"Hey, there you guys are."

The voice had them both spinning. Lars stepped through the doorway of the building.

Peri smiled. "We are *so* glad to see you. We had an incident, but we're okay."

Beside her, she sensed Ronin stiffen a little. His gaze was scanning behind Lars.

"Where are Dec and Logan?" Ronin asked.

"We lost your trail. They went to check one direction, and I came this way."

Peri nodded, but when she looked over at Ronin, she detected something from him that she didn't understand. "What's wrong?"

Lars shook his head. "You have some sharp instincts, Coop." The scientist pulled out a pistol and aimed it at Ronin.

Peri gasped. "What the hell are you doing?"

"I'm afraid your expedition ends here." There was regret on the man's face, but his arm didn't waver.

"They offered you money," Ronin said. "What is it? Sick kid? Relative in debt?"

"Sick wife," Lars answered sadly. "She has cancer, and the doctors back home can't do any more for her. But there's an experimental treatment in Germany." He shot Peri a regretful look. "I'm so sorry, Peri. I didn't have the money, and I need to save my wife."

Peri swallowed hard, betrayal cutting through her. "Did you kill your colleagues, too?"

"No!" There was horror on his face. "But I was supposed to keep all the station people away from Silk Road, and what they were doing here. Unfortunately, two of them ignored my warnings."

God, this couldn't be happening. Peri pressed her hands to her thighs. "You attacked me. In the bathroom."

Heat filled Lars' cheeks. "I'm sorry about that."

Ronin took a threatening step forward. "You choked her."

"Stay back." The man's gun stayed steady.

"Dec and Logan?" Ronin's tone was as sharp as a blade.

Lars cleared his throat. "I'm sorry, I—"

Ronin leaped forward so fast, Peri jerked in shock. He landed a hard chop to Lars' arm, and the scientist cried out, his gun hitting the icy floor. Ronin gripped the front of the man's coat, and jerked him around. A hard punch to Lars' face snapped the man's head back and blood spurted from his nose.

"You couldn't have killed Dec and Logan," Ronin said. "They would've seen you coming a mile away."

"No." Lars pressed a gloved hand to his nose. "But the last I saw of them, they were in an unstable area. Ice was falling down from the roof, all around them."

Ronin's hand struck out, his fist slamming into Lars' temple. The man crashed into the wall and slumped down to the floor, out cold. Ronin reached down and picked up the pistol. "We need to move. We need to find Dec and Logan."

With a nod, Peri hitched the straps of her backpack tighter, and clicked her flashlight on. She followed Ronin out of the warehouse.

Then, she heard Ronin make a sound.

Before she could respond, a jolt of electricity raced through her body. Pain hit her, and her body started jerking. She collapsed on the ice.

*Hurts. So. Bad.* She forced herself to move her head slightly, trying to see what was happening around her. The ice was cold on her bare cheek. *What was going on?*

Ahead, she saw Ronin fall heavily to his knees, his teeth clenched, and his body jerking.

She blinked slowly, and that's when she saw the small prongs in his back, and the thin wires protruding from them. Taser. *Damn.*

Heavy, black boots stepped in front of her face, crunching on the ice. But before she could see who'd attacked them, she passed out from the pain.

## CHAPTER THIRTEEN

R onin rose out of the black fog of unconsciousness, his entire body aching. *Fuck.* He kept his eyes closed, his brain whirling, trying to piece things back together. *Peri!*

Fighting off the pain, he opened his eyes a crack. Where the hell was Peri?

Unfamiliar panic rose, but then he saw her still-unconscious body beside his. He moved his hand close to her face and felt the warm puff of her breath on his skin. He released a breath. She was alive.

He shifted a little to scan the space around them. They were back in the main part of the old warehouse. Several men and one woman—all in black, cold-weather gear, and armed—stood nearby, talking quietly. Typical Silk Road muscle.

"You're awake."

The voice behind Ronin had an Australian accent. He swiveled his head and spotted a man crouching down, his hands dangling between his knees. He had an open, handsome face, with shaggy, blond hair escaping the black winter hat he wore.

"We were surprised to find you in our city," the man said.

Ronin sat up. "Who are you?" His voice was a little croaky. He hated being hit with a Taser.

"My name is Jesse Colston. This is my expedition."

"So you're a thief."

"Yep. And you're Ronin Cooper. Treasure Hunter Pain-in-the-ass Security." The man's smile was slow and easy. "Did you find the vajra?"

Ronin's pulse tripped. They hadn't found it yet. "The weapon you're looking for?"

Colston nodded thoughtfully. "You don't have it. You would've rubbed it in my face if you had, I'm certain."

Beside Ronin, Peri stirred. She rose up on one elbow, her gaze landing blearily on Colston. Her eyes widened, and she sat bolt upright. "You!"

"Ah, Miss Butler." Colston shook his head. "You were stupid to come down here."

Peri glanced around, her worried gaze meeting Ronin's before she looked back at the Silk Road man. "Where's my sister?"

"She's proven herself very useful," Colston said.

Peri's lips firmed. "Is she alive?"

The man nodded. "For now. Who else is with you?"

They both stayed silent. Then Colston moved, faster than Ronin had expected. He grabbed a handful of Peri's jacket and jerked her to her feet.

Ronin leaped up and took a step toward the man. He wanted to slam a fist in the guy's surfer-boy face.

Ronin heard the guards move, and froze. Out of the corner of his eye, he saw several of them pointing assault rifles in his direction.

"Who. Else?" Colston said, giving Peri a shake.

"Fuck you." Her voice was soaked with venom.

Colston nodded his head. A guard stepped forward and punched Ronin in the lower back. *Dammit*, right in the kidneys. He arched his back and swallowed a groan. He wouldn't give Colston the satisfaction. Peri bit down on her lip.

"There are two others," a male voice said.

Ronin looked over at Lars, sitting against the rock wall. He had his knees drawn up, a hand probing his swollen, bloody nose. "Declan Ward and Logan O'Connor."

Colston's expression turned very unhappy. "Dammit all to hell." He shoved Peri away from him. "Declan Fucking Ward is here. That's all I need."

Ronin caught Peri, and her hands twisted in his jacket. Staying calm, he studied the group, taking in size, strength, and weapons. He *had* to protect Peri. He had to get her out of here.

He scanned their surroundings, his gaze landing on an open doorway that led outside of the warehouse. If they could get out onto the street, they could lose themselves in the maze of buildings, and hopefully lose Silk Road.

He looked down at Peri, and saw she was watching

him. He inclined his head minutely to the doorway. She blinked slowly.

*Good girl.* Now, they just needed a chance.

"Damn, just what I fucking needed," Colston ground out. "Declan Ward breathing down my neck. For once, I thought we'd managed to avoid THS, and—"

Before the man could finish his rant, Ronin reared forward and head-butted him. The Australian let out a shout, and Ronin swung him around, using him as a shield between Peri and him, and the rest of the group.

"Go!" he yelled at Peri.

"Don't shoot!" Colston shouted.

Peri took off, sprinting for the door. Ronin gave Colston a shove, and then followed her.

Gunfire echoed off the walls and bullets pinged off the ice nearby. Ronin ducked and dived out of the doorway.

He was back on his feet in an instant, grabbing Peri's arm. "Run."

They quickly turned the corner, their boots slapping on the slick, rocky ground.

"Get them!" a male voice boomed.

"Which way did they go?"

Holding on tight to Peri, Ronin sprinted down the streets, twisting and turning. A flurry of gunfire followed behind. Bullets slammed into the ice beside them with a thick thud.

"Down that alley," he called to Peri.

She adjusted her course, but when more gunfire sounded, she stumbled and crashed into him.

He caught her, half carrying her into the relative safety of the alley.

*Fuck, was she hit?* "Are you okay? Did they get you?"

She slapped a hand over her arm, and then tugged at her jacket. "Bullet winged me."

He gently turned her arm around. He saw a tear in her jacket, but no blood.

"I'm fine, Ronin."

*Thank God.* The sound of shouts and footsteps grew closer. "Come on."

They took off running again. They sprinted between two buildings, and out into a large square. It was ringed by ice-coated buildings and the center was a solid sheet of ice.

All the buildings and doorways nearby were glued together with ice. There might have been streets between them, but they were impassable.

It was a fucking dead end. They were trapped.

The voices behind them were getting louder.

"Across there." Peri pointed to the far side of the square.

Ronin looked and spotted a place where a hole had been smashed through an ice wall. Cracks radiated outward.

"Go!" He pulled her across the square.

"Shit." She almost slipped, her leg sliding out wildly from beneath her.

The ice here was extra slick, forcing them to slow their breakneck pace.

"Stop them!" someone shouted behind them.

Ronin heard gunfire again. *Dammit.*

Then he heard something far worse.

*Crack.*

The ground beneath their feet tilted. Peri yelped and threw her arms out for balance. All around them, the ground became a web of cracks, and then a split-second later, the ice broke apart.

Ronin shifted his weight to keep his balance.

"God, this must have been a small lake or pond that iced over," she said.

There were startled shouts behind them, and Ronin glanced back. Several Silk Road members had followed them out onto the ice.

Cracking noises echoed through the air as the ice continued to break up between them and Silk Road. The ice shifted again and he pulled Peri close. They were currently standing on a large piece that was slowly drifting across the icy water.

He remembered the shock of hitting the water earlier. He *really* didn't want to take another dip, and he sure as hell wasn't going to let Peri fall.

Behind them, he heard one of the Silk Road men scream, followed by a splash.

Ronin's jaw clenched. "We have to keep moving."

---

PERI STARED across the icy pool. "It's not too far to the edge."

Ronin looked grim as he studied the ice ahead of them. There were several stepping stones of decent-sized ice sheets that created a makeshift path to the side.

*Bang. Bang. Bang.* Peri flinched and ducked. She felt a bullet whiz past, not too far from her head. Both she and Ronin dropped down to the ice.

"Let's jump to the next one," she said.

He nodded. Peri dragged in a deep breath and stood. Blocking out the sounds of Silk Road behind her, she took two steps, and leaped over the water. She landed on the next sheet of ice, her arms windmilling, trying to keep her balance. Her feet skidded, and she dropped to her stomach to stop her slide.

Ronin landed right beside her in a crouch, and set the ice sheet rocking.

Once it had stopped, he helped her up. "Again."

They jumped the thankfully short distance to the next sheet. Then the next.

The fourth ice sheet moved under their weight, sliding across the cold water. They held on to each other, dropping to their knees. Peri put her few surfing skills to use, trying to hold her balance.

She risked a glance back. The Silk Road members were following them, leaping from ice sheet to ice sheet.

"Peri! Ronin!"

She saw Lars balanced precariously on some ice.

"Stop before they kill you," the man called out.

"He still thinks they'll let him go," she murmured to Ronin.

"Yes, but they won't."

The next second, Lars slipped, and with a sharp cry, he landed in the water with a splash. For a second, Peri felt sorry for him. A formerly decent man corrupted.

"Let's go. That one over there." Ronin nodded at the next piece of ice.

Shoving thoughts of Lars out of her head, she studied the next closest ice sheet. It was far smaller than the previous ones. She swallowed. There were no larger ones close enough to reach.

He squeezed her arm. "You can do it. I've never met a more determined woman than you."

Peri felt a flush of heat. She nodded and focused on her target.

She jumped, and when she landed, the ice teetered wildly. The sheet tilted up, and she flailed, her heart lodged in her throat. She was going to fall in—

Ronin landed solidly beside her, sending the ice sheet tilting back the other way. He wrapped his arms around her and she grabbed onto him.

They steadied each other. *Hell.* She blew out a breath.

"Nearly there," he said.

There was more gunfire, but she blocked it out. Only one more ice sheet to go, and from that, they could reach the far edge of the pond.

"One more," she muttered, encouraging herself.

More shouts and a splash came from behind them. Spurred on, Peri leaped over to the next sheet. She ducked down and waited for Ronin.

He landed in a crouch. They both stared across to the edge. This gap was larger than all the other jumps. Peri backed up as far she could, ran, and threw herself into the air. She tossed her arms over her head, and brought them down, trying to buy herself every bit of momentum she could.

Her boot hit the edge and she tipped forward, smacking onto solid rock. The wind was knocked out of her, and she lay there for a moment, seriously considering kissing the ground, except she was afraid her lips would stick.

Ronin landed beside her with a graceful roll. He shot back to his feet, grabbed her hand, and yanked her up.

"Keep moving." He stopped at the hole in the ice wall.

It looked like a giant had punched a hole through it. Recently.

"Who the hell made this?" he said.

She glanced back. The Silk Road team was most of the way across the pond. "No time." She ducked through the hole.

A street opened ahead. There were several open-air buildings here and she frowned. She could see long benches, frozen in ice, under the structures. Workshops, maybe.

"We need to put as much distance between us and Silk Road as we can." Ronin took her hand.

As they set off down the street, she saw several round features flanking the road, circled by low stone walls. She paused at one and glanced down.

"Oh." She jerked back. "Watch out. These are holes." It reminded her far too starkly of the hole Ronin had fallen in earlier. "Deep ones."

Ronin gripped her hand. "Wells, maybe. Or for waste."

"Probably wise to avoid them."

They broke into a jog, staying clear of the wells. Peri realized how well they moved together. He shortened his stride to match hers, their bodies brushing occasionally, but never getting in each other's way.

They rounded a corner. With a sharp gasp, Peri skidded to a halt.

Ronin muttered a curse.

Several people stood in a row ahead of them, all clad in black cold-weather gear. They had guns aimed at Peri and Ronin.

A tall woman pushed forward, frowning at them. She had pale skin and dark hair pulled back off her strong features. She moved with an imperious air, like she was used to giving orders. "Who the fuck are you?"

Her accent was very sharp and very British. Peri studied her. She looked familiar.

Then Peri spied another woman, slightly hidden behind the group. A woman with copper-colored hair and a bruised face. "Amber!"

Peri watched her sister's head shoot up, and her blue eyes—a few shades lighter than Peri's—widened. Amber's face turned stricken. "Peri? What are you doing here?"

All of a sudden, there were more shouts from behind them. Peri glanced back and saw Jesse Colston leading his group up behind them. *Damn.*

Colston stomped forward, a smug expression on his face. "Vicky, I see you've met our guests. Treasure Hunter Security."

A grimace crossed the woman's face. "Do not call me

that ridiculous name. I hate it almost as much as I hate uninvited guests."

Peri recognized the woman now. "You're some distant member of the British royal family."

The woman sniffed. "Lady Victoria Eugenie Alexandra Armstrong-Jones. And I'm not that distant. I'm twelfth in line to the throne."

"And you're one of the leaders of Silk Road," Ronin said.

Peri blinked. This woman, probably the same age as Peri, *ran* Silk Road.

Lady Victoria raised her arm, pointing her pistol straight at Ronin's chest. "You needn't concern yourself with that."

There was no emotion on the woman's face now, and fear skated down Peri's spine. Whatever else this woman was, she was dangerous.

# CHAPTER FOURTEEN

R onin kept his face impassive as his arms were jerked roughly behind him.

He'd run out of options and ideas. Hell, he'd even take a bad option at this stage. He looked at Peri, and saw her glaring at the Silk Road people. Then, she cast a worried glance at her sister.

Amber Butler was a slightly taller, sharper version of her sister. She wore her copper-colored hair longer than Peri, and had paler eyes. Right now, she looked tired and dejected.

"There are two more THS men here, as well," Colston said. "One of them is Declan Ward."

Lady Victoria shook her head. "Bloody hell. We need to find and secure the weapon." She skewered her team with a hard look. "I brought the best linguistics expert in the world down here. Why the hell can't we find the damn vajra?"

A small, slight man cleared his throat. He was

wearing a pair of round glasses which he pushed up his nose, and was dwarfed by his bulky coat. "I translated the standing-stone glyphs." He had an Indian accent. "It isn't my fault you can't interpret the location correctly."

"What is this weapon?" Ronin demanded. They might be dead soon, and he sure as hell wanted to know what he was dying for.

The Silk Road leader turned, eyeing him with a narrow gaze. Her eyes were a bright hazel color. "The vajra is an indestructible weapon of a god, with the power of a thunderbolt." She smiled. "Actually, our scientists believe it is a powerful, portable, reusable nuclear weapon."

*Fuck.* Ronin stared at the woman. What the hell did Silk Road hope to achieve? Use the weapon? See it sold to the highest bidder? His gut churned with the hellish possibilities.

"You won't get away with it," Peri said.

"Says the woman with a gun to her head." Lady Victoria raised a plucked brow. "Silk Road will continue finding artifacts and solidify our power base and wealth. Now, I want that weapon found!" She looked at the linguist. "Tell me what the stone said again."

The man lifted a tablet and repeated his translation. "Here lies a terrible power, the city its tomb, this message its guardian," the man said. "A terrible power that shook the world in a single flash of light. Do not enter here, for you will find nothing but death."

Ronin realized they were a more detailed version of the words on the stone in the central square of the city.

"There must be more clues to the vajra's resting place," Lady Victoria said.

The linguist straightened. "I stand by my translation."

Ronin saw Peri's lips moving, then her eyes widened, and she tried to stifle a gasp.

Lady Victoria and Colston swiveled. "You thought of something?" the woman said.

"I...we couldn't read the full translation," Peri said.

Lady Victoria strode up to Peri and grabbed her arm. "And you've noticed something we haven't?"

"No—" Peri shook her head.

The woman spun, her gaze settling on Ronin. "Bring him over here."

Two men shoved and dragged Ronin over to one of the holes in the ground. They pushed him up onto the small stone wall and held him at the very edge. He looked down at the narrow well, into the yawning darkness below.

"No!" Peri struggled against her guards.

"Tell me," Lady Victoria ordered. "Or Mr. Cooper has a very long drop."

"Okay." Peri wrenched free and straightened. "It's probably nothing."

"Don't say anything, Peri," he said.

She shot him a hot look. "*Here* lies a terrible power, and the message is its *guardian*."

Lady Victoria frowned. "So?"

"And 'do not enter for you will find *nothing* but death.' It sounds like the vajra is in or below the message stone. The stone is guarding it and if you go beyond it, you'll find nothing."

The Silk Road woman's brows shot up. "So bloody simple."

Colston grinned. "This is it!"

"Please leave Ronin alone," Peri said.

Lady Victoria's nose wrinkled. "No, I don't think so."

*Damn.* Ronin knew he should have seen this coming.

"He's dangerous," Lady Victoria added.

"So what will we do with them?" a guard asked.

The woman waved a hand. "Kill them."

*No.* "Wait!" Ronin struggled against his captors. "Peri just helped you." He'd do anything to keep her alive. Bright, beautiful Peri, who'd shone a light into the darkness inside him. He wouldn't see that brightness extinguished. "And she's an experienced guide, like her sister. She can help you get out of here."

Peri's brows drew together. "Ronin—"

"The man has a point," Lady Victoria said. "The woman comes, but kill him."

"No!" Peri lunged toward Ronin, but two guards grabbed her, dragging her back. She kicked one and the man grunted.

Ronin kept his gaze on her. "Peri." There was so much that he wanted to say to her...and now he'd never get the chance. Damn, he should have manned up and admitted he was falling for her.

She shoved against the men holding her. "Ronin! Don't—"

One of Ronin's guards shoved him in the chest, knocking him into the well.

As Ronin fell, slick ice walls rushing past him, he heard Peri's wild scream.

---

PERI FOUGHT AGAINST HER GUARDS. *Ronin. No. No. No.*

Distraught, she managed to knock one of her guards to the ground. They'd taken her man away. A good, solid man. The man she was falling for.

*Gone.* He was gone. Her stomach tightened to a hard point, a horrible sensation growing inside her.

Slim arms wrapped around Peri, and she smelled her sister.

"Shh, Peri. I'm here."

"They killed him." A hollow feeling spread through Peri. They'd killed the man who was coming to mean everything to her. A man who'd stood by her side since this terrible situation had started. A man who'd filled a part of her that she hadn't even realized was empty.

With a sob, Peri turned to her sister, and wrapped her arms around Amber. Behind them, she heard the Silk Road people planning the path back to the central square and standing stone. But Peri just focused on breathing through her pain. She felt hot and cold, her chest impossibly tight. Even though her chest heaved, tears didn't come. It was like they were locked up inside her.

"Hey." Amber smoothed Peri's hair back. "Hey, sis, just focus on me. Lock it away. Like we did when we were kids, and we'd have to leave our friends and move to a new place."

Peri looked at her sister. Amber's face was bruised and there was a nasty cut on her left cheekbone. Peri pulled in a shaky breath. For now, she needed to focus on Amber and how to get them out of there alive. She glanced at the well, and pain rocketed through her. She wanted to scream, and throw herself at Victoria Armstrong-Jones and scratch the woman's eyes out.

But Peri locked it down, just like she had in the past. She locked her feelings for Ronin deep inside. She turned her attention completely back to her sister.

She cupped Amber's cheek. "Are you okay?"

Amber nodded, biting her lip. "It's just scratches and bruises. You were right, sis. I should never have come down here."

Peri grabbed Amber's hand and squeezed. "We need to focus on getting out of here." *Alive.*

"Let's move out," Lady Victoria shouted, interrupting their quiet moment.

Peri and Amber were nudged forward. As they walked down the icy street, Peri cast one last glance at the well. Pain and grief poured into her, almost too much to bear.

Then she faced forward and tried to think of nothing.

"I'm sorry about your friend," her sister said quietly.

"I...was falling in love with him."

"Oh, God, Peri." Her sister hugged her again.

"Keep moving," a guard barked from the rear.

"All right. Everyone move fast, and keep up," Colston shouted. "And if you see anyone else in here that doesn't belong with us, shoot them."

They walked through streets, passed through buildings, skirted squares. Peri just focused on putting one foot in front of the other, not paying attention to where they were going.

Finally, the buildings opened up, and they stepped once more into the large central square. Immediately, Lady Victoria made a beeline to the massive standing stone in the center.

The rest of them followed her, finally stopping in front of the ancient sentinel, the group fanning out.

The Silk Road woman lifted her chin. "Rogers, bring the explosives. Blow it open."

Peri gasped. They were going to blow up a piece of ancient history. She and Amber were hustled out of the way, a guard standing over them.

The Silk Road team worked fast and a second later, they scrambled back.

"It's ready to blow," someone shouted.

Peri hugged Amber, pressing her face against her sister's hair. There was a huge muffled *thwomp* and the floor shook.

When Peri lifted her head, the standing stone was now pieces of rubble on the icy floor.

Lady Victoria and Colston hurried over, picking through the chunks of rock.

"Oh, my God," the woman breathed.

Colston gave an excited whoop and several guards laughed.

Peri swallowed and watched Lady Victoria pick up something metallic. It was about the length of the woman's forearm.

She held it up, smiling widely. "The vajra!"

It looked exactly as Dec had described it—a metallic rod, with what looked like claws at the end. It was copper-colored.

As Peri stared at it, a spike of emotion shot through her. Ronin would not have let this artifact fall into Silk Road's hands.

Lady Victoria carefully wrapped the ancient weapon in a cloth and slipped it into her backpack. She settled the bag on her back. "All right, you two—" she pointed at Peri and Amber "—get us out of here. Fast."

Something unfurled in Peri. She stepped forward and nodded. The urge to jump on the woman and choke her was strong, but she held it back. "I can get us out of here. I even know a shortcut." She pointed. "That way."

Lady Victoria inclined her head. "Good. Let's move."

Peri took the lead, keeping Amber close beside her. "Stay close to me." She kept her voice to a whisper.

"I know that look, Peri—" Her sister's voice was shaky.

"Trust me."

"Always."

Peri led Silk Road on a fast clip through the city. She stared hard at the landmarks, and old tracks from earlier. She was certain they were heading in the right direction.

Ahead, she spotted the area where the ice had come in and formed the ice cavern. The blue-green colors were so beautiful.

"This is the shortcut," she called back. "The ground's rough, so move fast and stay together."

As she stepped inside the cavern, she prayed no one

looked up. "When I say run, you run," she whispered to her sister. "And stay close to the side wall."

Amber's eyes widened, but she nodded.

Peri led them into the large cavern. She glanced back once to assess the group, and fought back a smirk of satisfaction. Everyone was so focused on navigating the rough, icy ground, that they didn't look up.

Slowly, Peri angled herself and Amber closer to the side wall. It was a gorgeous sweep of ice. *Keep moving, keep moving.*

Peri looked back again. The Silk Road team members were all slipping and cursing as they crossed the cavern. They were also bunched perfectly in a group in the center of the space.

*Perfect.* "Come on." She raised her voice. "Everyone keep up!"

One icicle fell. It slammed down, shattering on the ground beside one of the Silk Road guards.

As the man screamed, more icicles shook loose, and started falling like a deadly rain of spikes.

"Run," Peri said to Amber.

The more panicked noise the group made, the more the dangerous spikes fell.

Peri focused on running as fast as she could, staying close to the wall. Amber was right behind her, and Silk Road's screams echoed behind them.

An icicle crashed into the ice just a few feet from Peri. She jerked to a halt, gesturing to Amber. They both pressed their bodies flat against the wall.

"We're almost out of here." Peri could see the exit not far away. "Keep going."

Together, they shimmied along the wall, blocking out the thumps and screams. They stumbled out into the street.

Amber was breathing fast. She looked back into the cavern. "Some of them made it through!"

Peri grabbed her sister's hand. "Let's go. Fast."

They sprinted down the street. Ahead, the street split, with one side climbing to an upper level of the city. Peri turned that way and they ran up the incline.

Without warning, there was the roar of gunfire. Bullets peppered the ground just behind them. *Shit.* Peri lunged to the side, pumping her arms. "Faster, Amber."

Amber cried out.

*No!* Peri skidded and turned. She saw her sister down on the ground, a hand pressed to her calf.

"Oh, my God, Peri, I got shot." Amber was breathing hard and fast.

Peri dropped down beside her sister. She could see the ragged tear in the fabric and the blood soaking her trousers.

Amber sat up and tried to stand. She dropped back with a grimace of pain. "I can't put any weight on it."

Peri's gut was as hard as rock. "I'll help you!"

"I'll never make it. Go, Peri. Get out!"

"I will *never* leave you." She'd already lost Ronin. She wasn't losing her sister, as well.

The remnants of the Silk Road team crested the ramp, Lady Victoria and Colston in the lead. The Silk Road leader's face didn't look attractive now. Anger was etched on the woman's features. She lifted her pistol and strode closer. She pressed the barrel right to the center of Peri's forehead.

Peri flinched. Lady Victoria looked disheveled now. Her arm was bleeding, and her coat ripped.

Colston stood behind the woman. He wasn't injured, but he looked pissed. It was clear they'd lost a lot of people in the ice cavern.

"Bitch." He shoved forward, grabbed a handful of Peri's jacket, and yanked her up. He dragged her over to the edge of the upper level. From here, she had a perfect view of the empty ice city below. He pushed her to the very edge, her foot slipping into midair.

"If I had a fucking well to drop you down like your dead boyfriend, I would. I'd listen to your screams echo around me."

"Fuck you," she spat.

"You made a bad choice, Ms. Butler."

"I'd do it again if I could."

"Peri!" Amber screamed. "Let her go."

Colston leaned closer. "Is your heart beating hard? Is fear burning in your gut?"

He shoved her again and Peri felt the empty space yawning behind her. She looked down. It was a long drop and she knew she wouldn't survive it.

"That's what Cooper was feeling as he fell in that hole." Colston's eyes glittered.

*Ronin.* Pain speared her chest, but she glared at Colston defiantly. She wouldn't give the bastard the pleasure of seeing her fear or pain. "Are you going to talk me to death, or what, Colston?"

He made an angry sound and pushed her over the edge.

Peri fell backward, seeing Colston and two other Silk Road thugs watching her as she fell. She heard Amber's screams.

Air rushed past Peri and she closed her eyes. She thought of Ronin's intense, not-quite-handsome face. The feel of his hard arms around her. The taste of his lips on hers.

Suddenly, she was caught in strong arms, the force of the fall knocking her and her rescuer to the ground and sending them sliding across the ice. Every bit of air was forced out of her lungs and she heard a masculine grunt beneath her.

When they came to a stop, she blinked. God, she was alive.

She turned her head to look at her savior and her chest locked up solid.

## CHAPTER FIFTEEN

"Peri? Are you okay?"

Ronin held Peri clutched tightly in his arms. She was staring at him with wide, disbelieving eyes.

"Ronin?" Her hands clamped on his cheeks. "Are we dead?"

He smiled. "No."

Understanding dawned on her beautiful features, then she burst into movement. She leaped at him, straddling his hips. She kissed him desperately, her hands moving all over him, like she was trying to make sure he was really there.

"You're alive?" she whispered.

"Yes."

She burst into heartbreaking sobs.

God, she was killing him. He wrapped his arms around her and pulled her into his chest. He murmured to her, stroking her back. "I'm here, baby. I'm sorry I had to leave you for a little while."

The sound of a throat being cleared caught Ronin's attention, and he looked over to where Logan and Dec stood. Dec was grinning and Logan was staring upward.

Ronin slid a hand around to the base of Peri's neck and squeezed. Her sobs morphed to quiet tears.

"I'm okay," he told her.

"How?" she asked in a watery voice. "I saw them push you into that hole." Her chest hitched.

He imagined if their situation were reversed, and he'd been forced to watch her fall and thought she was dead, he'd feel the same as her. He tightened his hold on her. Watching that bastard Colston push her off the damn cliff had been bad enough.

"The well was narrow. I threw my arms and legs out and managed to slow my slide. Then I clung there and tried to work out a plan." He didn't tell her that his muscles had been burning and shaking, and he'd been close to sliding down into oblivion. "Dec and Logan had been watching us. After Silk Road left, they arrived and pulled me out."

As soon as he'd gotten out, he'd raced off, desperate to find Peri.

She kissed him again, fiercely, tears still streaming down her cheeks. "I love you."

Shock made him go still.

"I don't care if you're a dark, dangerous loner. I don't care if you don't know about love. You're mine, and I'll teach you all about it until you love me back. Until you worship the ground I walk on." Her tone was ferocious.

He sank his hands into her hair, emotions filling his

chest. He wasn't sure what each part of the tangle was, but he knew where they all ended. "Okay."

She tilted her head. "Okay? That's all you've got to say after telling me you aren't the love and togetherness kind of guy?"

Ronin smiled. "I doubt it'll take me long to learn how to love you, Peri. I think I'm already on my way."

She made a sound, her face softening. Their kiss this time was slower, more tender.

The sound of a clearing throat came again. "Bad guys with a dangerous artifact are getting away," Dec said. "And we need to rescue Peri's sister."

Peri jolted and looked up. Ronin nodded. "Ready to go?"

She nodded.

"Let's go get your sister and save the world."

"No pressure." She pushed to her feet, nodding at Dec and Logan. "Glad you guys are okay."

"You, too," Dec said.

"Silk Road will be heading out of here in the quickest direction possible," she said.

"We'll stop them," Ronin said darkly.

"There aren't too many of them left," she said with savage satisfaction.

Ronin smiled. "Saw you lead them through that icicle cavern."

"I'd do it again if I could."

"Really don't ever want to get on your bad side."

"All right, let's go," Dec said.

They headed off, following the trail of the Silk Road team. It wasn't long before they heard voices ahead.

Dec held up a hand and they huddled together. "Logan and I will circle around. You guys attack them from the rear. Start picking off the guards and take down as many as you can."

Ronin nodded. "Got it." He pulled out the spare Glock Dec had given him and checked it.

"Let's end this and secure the weapon," Dec said. "Good luck." He and Logan slipped between two buildings and disappeared.

"Will you stay back?" Ronin asked Peri quietly.

"Hell, no."

He sighed. He'd known she'd say that. And hell, Peri had proven over and over that she could handle herself. He pulled out the combat knife Logan had given him and handed it to her. "Take this."

She gripped it and nodded.

"And stay close to me."

They crept down along the side of a building. Around the corner, they heard voices, and he realized that Silk Road had stopped to rest.

"Hey, where's Chang?" someone said.

"He went around that way."

"The idiot fucking wandered off. We need to stick together."

"He'll be back."

Or not. Looked like Dec and Logan had started taking down the guards.

Ronin moved up to the end of the wall, his back pressed to the rock. He carefully glanced around the wall and pulled back. In that split second, he'd taken in the number of guards and their locations.

"Two heading this way," he murmured to Peri. She lifted her knife.

He slowed his breathing. *Time to attack.*

---

TWO SILK ROAD guards rounded the corner. They were talking and laughing, not paying any attention.

Before Peri even planned a response, Ronin attacked.

*God.* He moved hard and fast. He grabbed the first guard and tossed him against the wall. With lethal, dangerous moves, he struck out, kicking the second guard in the knee. The man went down and Ronin was on him in a second. He gripped the man's neck and twisted. The cracking sound made her wince.

He flowed upward, just as the second guard shook his head and focused on Ronin. Three hard, short punches and the guard went down.

This was what Ronin thought was all he had to offer. The violence, the fighting, being a shield for the people he considered good and innocent.

But there was so much more to him. Courage, an unshakable sense of right and wrong, and the bravery to do the things others didn't want to do in order to protect.

He looked at her. "Okay?"

She moved to him and pressed a quick kiss to his lips. "Yes."

Something moved in his eyes.

"Rogers, where the hell are—" A man rounded the corner.

He stared at them in shock, took one step back, and

opened his mouth to alert the others.

Peri ran forward. She swung out with the knife and stabbed him in the belly.

The man grunted, and they both stared at each other for a horrible second. He started to fall backward, just as another guard appeared. This one was holding a dangerous-looking, black rifle.

His gaze narrowed and he started to raise the weapon. Without thinking, Peri dropped down, sliding on the ice, and kicked the legs out from under him.

He fell on his back with a shout. Before Peri could get to her feet, Ronin rushed past her like a blurred, dark bullet. He slammed down on the man, and, with a hard blow, knocked the Silk Road man out.

Ronin snatched up the rifle and stood.

Peri heard shouts. Silk Road knew they were here.

All of a sudden, a female scream echoed off the ice around them. Peri's head snapped up, her heart kicking against her ribs. "Amber."

"Come out now and I won't kill her," Colston called out.

Peri stared at Ronin.

"Now!" Colston roared.

Peri didn't hesitate. She stepped around the corner, and Ronin was right behind her.

Colston stood with only four guards. He had Amber clutched in front of him, a pistol pressed to her temple. "Drop your weapons."

Peri tossed her knife and it clattered to the ice. Ronin set the rifle down on the ground.

"THS is such a fucking pain in my ass. You guys just

won't die." Colston's face screwed up. "I'm getting out of here with the vajra. You won't fucking stop me."

Ronin raised a brow. "The weapon your partner seems to have taken off with?"

Colston blinked. He turned his head to look behind him.

There was no sign of Lady Victoria.

"Victoria? *Vicky*?" A muscle ticked in his jaw. He pressed the gun harder against Amber's skin and she moaned. Then he cursed.

"I don't actually think honor amongst thieves exists," Ronin said.

"Shut up! I'll kill you, and your woman, and that traitorous bitch I've had to pander to."

Peri stared at the angry man, her mind whirling as she tried to work out what Ronin's plan was. He looked composed and relaxed, despite the guns aimed at them.

"We both know Victoria will be long gone," Ronin said.

"I said, shut up." Spittle flew from Colston's mouth. The easygoing man and his cool surfer persona were long gone.

That's when Peri spotted a flash of movement. She made sure she didn't look in that direction, but out of the corner of her eye, she saw Logan's big form sneaking up behind the Silk Road team.

Ronin was keeping Colston distracted so he didn't notice.

She could help with that. "Amber, are you okay?"

Her sister bit her lip, terror on her face. "No."

"It'll be okay," Peri promised.

"Oh?" Colston dragged Amber closer. "I'm the one with the gun, so how do you figure that?"

"Because you're surrounded by pissed off former Navy SEALs," Peri said, wild satisfaction flaring inside her. "And the one behind you looks especially angry."

Colston and his men jerked, all starting to turn.

Logan attacked and Dec flew out of nowhere. They attacked the men with hard kicks. She saw Logan land an unforgiving blow to one of the guards. The guard staggered back into Colston. With a shout, Colston fell, Amber falling with him.

"Get your sister." Ronin leaped into the fight to help.

Peri darted in and grabbed Amber's arm. She pulled her sister out of the mêlée. "Amber!"

"God." Amber hugged her tightly.

Peri was aware of curses and grunts, and the dull thud of flesh striking flesh, as the fight continued around them.

"No!" Colston was trying to scramble away. Ronin grabbed the back of his jacket and hauled the man up.

"You threw my woman off a fucking cliff." Ronin's voice was low and lethal.

Goosebumps broke out on Peri's skin. Colston broke free and ran. Ronin pulled his Glock, aimed, and fired.

Colston hit the ice face first and didn't move.

Peri hugged her sister again. "Are you all right?"

Amber nodded, tears in her eyes. "I am now. Thanks for coming for me, sis."

"Let me see your leg," Peri said.

"It isn't too bad. Colston had someone patch it up."

Peri saw the blood-soaked bandage. It would have to

do for now. God, this nightmare was almost over. "Love you."

"Love you, too," Amber whispered.

Ronin appeared. "Everyone okay?"

Peri threw herself at him, burying her face in his neck. He held on tight, his hands flexing on her.

"Amber, this is Ronin. Ronin, my sister, Amber."

Amber smiled. "Hi."

"And the others are Declan and Logan." She leaned into Ronin's side. "They're with Treasure Hunter Security. I hired them to help me rescue you."

Dec appeared. "We need to stop the Silk Road woman and get the artifact."

Amber rubbed her sleeve across her face. "I noticed when she left. She went that way." Amber pointed down an empty street.

"Let's end this," Peri said.

---

VICTORIA WASN'T MAKING any effort to hide her tracks. She was just running as fast as she could.

Ronin skirted some rubble, studying the ground. They were closing in on her.

He glanced over at Peri, who was walking with her sister and helping support Amber. She looked like she'd been dragged through hell. Both women did. His chest tightened. He wanted this mission over, and wanted to get Peri out of here.

Then he thought about this assignment being over. His jaw worked. He still wasn't sure what kind of future he had with Peri. She'd opened him up, shone light into the dark parts of his soul. He didn't want to give her up. Ever. But he knew she deserved far better than him.

They turned onto another street, and ahead, he saw ice had infiltrated this area of the city. A huge wall of it blocked the way. Toward the top of it were some ledges and tunnel entrances.

Lady Victoria was at the base of the ice cliff looking up.

*Nowhere to go.* A slow smile curved Ronin's lips. "It's over, Vicky."

The woman spun to face them, her face tight and angry. "Damn you! You ruined everything."

Dec took a step forward. "I'm not planning to make your day any better. Hand over the vajra."

The Silk Road leader shook her head. "It doesn't matter if you kill me. The Collector will never stop."

"The Collector?" Dec asked with a frown.

"The true head of Silk Road." She smiled, and it wasn't pretty. "He'll see that you pay for everything THS has done. The Collector will break your business and your family apart, piece by piece." She lifted a hand, holding the artifact up. "And if I'm going to die, we can all go to hell together."

She gripped the vajra with both hands, touching something on it. Suddenly, a blinding light shot out of the device.

"What the hell?" Logan snarled.

Every muscle in Ronin went tight. *Hell.* He lunged toward Peri.

"She's activated the vajra!" Dec shouted.

## CHAPTER SIXTEEN

*uck.* Ronin raised his Glock. Beside him, Logan and Dec did the same. They all fired together.

But nothing reached the woman, the bullets disintegrating in the light.

It was so bright now, that tears streamed down Ronin's face. He didn't know what the hell the device really was, but if it was nuclear, there was nowhere they could run to escape it.

He dived on Peri. They slammed to the ice, and he wrapped himself around her.

"Ronin."

"I love you, Peri." He wasn't losing his chance to tell her.

Her fingers dug into him. "I love you, too."

Amber hunkered down near them, her face pale. Ronin heard Logan groan and Dec curse. When Ronin looked up, through the light he saw Logan had one arm tossed over his face. Dec was trying to move forward, his face contorted with pain.

Ronin tightened his hold on Peri. Shit, he'd failed her. He couldn't protect her from this.

*Thwap.* The sound cut through the air, and abruptly, the light was extinguished.

Confused, Ronin watched spots dance in front of his stinging eyes as they adjusted.

"Fucking hell." Logan's voice.

Ronin lifted his head. Victoria was flopping on the ground, caught in a heavy-duty, black net.

He looked up and saw a team of people standing on one of the ice ledges above. They were dressed in all-white, cold-weather gear, goggles pulled over their faces. One was holding a net-launcher device.

The team threw ropes down the ice wall and seconds later, were rappelling down.

Ronin pushed up, helping Peri to her feet. Her eyes were red and watery. The others all stood as well. They watched the team in white stride over to secure Victoria and the vajra.

"Amber?" Peri called out.

"I'm okay."

One man broke away from the group, and headed toward them. His cold-weather gear did nothing to hide the big, powerful body beneath. He moved like someone who had honed their body to be a weapon. He stopped and lifted his goggles up on top of his hood. The bottom half of his face was covered by a white bandana, so just his eyes were visible.

They were a deep amber color.

Dec stepped forward. "The team in black is the team in white today."

"Ward. Thanks for helping us locate a dangerous artifact."

"You mean weapon," Declan said.

The man in white shot Dec a hard stare. "It doesn't matter what it's called. I'm securing it."

"Target restrained." A woman in white came to stand behind the man.

"Who the hell are these people?" Peri demanded.

The man lifted a hand. With a start, Ronin realized the man wasn't wearing a glove and his skin was a bright, silver color. *No.* Ronin looked harder. The man had some sort of high-tech prosthetic.

"It's none of your concern, Ms. Butler." The man's voice was deep. "But I assure you, the artifact is in safe hands."

"And it'll be studied," Dec said with a scowl. "And reverse engineered."

"No," the man replied. "It will be *secured*. That's all I can tell you." He glanced at his team, then stepped back. "We'd be happy to give you a ride back to Aurora Station. We have a helicopter."

"We aren't giving them our find," Logan growled.

The man straightened. "I work for the government, Mr. O'Connor. Your government. I'm authorized to take the weapon in."

"You fuckers nearly killed Hale and Agent Alexander on the last mission we were involved in," Dec said.

Ronin was well aware Dec was still pissed about the drone incident in the Kalahari Desert.

"That was...a mistake."

"And maybe it's a mistake giving you this artifact, too," Logan said.

"Are you going to fight us for it?" the man asked in a silky tone.

Logan's hands curled into fists. "We could take you."

Ronin tensed, waiting to see what Dec wanted to do.

Dec sighed, looking tired. "You know what? I want a hot shower, a beer, and then a plane ride back to my wife. So sure. You want a dangerous artifact, it's yours."

"I fucking hate these guys," Logan grumbled.

"You did good work today. This could have ended badly." The man's gaze connected with Declan's. "I'm not authorized to tell you this, but we're called Team 52."

Dec raised a brow. "Which tells me nothing."

Ronin got the distinct impression the man was smiling behind his bandana.

"It beats 'the team in white' or 'the team in black'," the man said.

Peri grabbed Ronin's hand. "It's over?" Her gaze moved to her sister, love and relief on her face.

"Yeah." He pulled Peri tight against his side. "Time to go home."

The Team 52 woman stepped toward them, also moving in a way that implied she could kill with very little effort. Ronin knew advanced combat training when he saw it.

"I'm sorry, but you'll need to hand over all recording

devices, and any images you've taken." Her voice was crisp and no-nonsense.

"I really want a hot shower and some pain relievers," Amber said with a moan. "And a triple-shot latte."

Peri squeezed her sister's arm before she turned and pressed her face against Ronin's chest. "I want to sleep for two days straight." She leaned into him and lowered her voice. "Care to join me?"

She'd soon learn that whatever she wanted, whatever she asked of him, the answer would always be the same. "Yes."

The trip out of the frozen city went fast with Team 52 escorting them.

Soon, they were walking across the snow in the weak Antarctic sunlight toward a sleek, white helicopter. The damn thing wasn't like anything Ronin had seen before and highly modified.

Ronin helped Peri and Amber inside and they settled in the seats in back. Up front, another white-suited soldier wearing a mirrored helmet raised a hand in welcome, but didn't say anything.

Ronin sat and slung an arm around Peri. She snuggled into him, her gaze on her sister, who had already buckled up and closed her eyes.

Logan slammed the side door closed. Moments later, they lifted off.

Ronin stared out the window. He watched the members of the mysterious Team 52 walking around the entrance down into the tunnels beneath the pyramid. But seconds later, they blended in with the ice and snow, and were gone. Then, he stared at the peak of the pyramid until it, too, disappeared from sight.

"We'll never hear anything about this city, will we?" Peri whispered. "All that history will be buried."

Across from them, Dec shrugged. "Maybe. Maybe not."

"There's important unknown history down there," Peri said. "History the world should know about."

Ronin leaned forward, sliding a hand into his pocket. Making sure his moves were hidden from the pilot, he slid out a small memory card and discreetly showed it to Peri. "Good thing I'm sneaky and very good at hiding things."

Peri laughed, a warm sound he'd never get tired of hearing. The others chuckled as well.

"What about the vajra?" Peri asked.

Dec sat back against his seat, crossing his hands over his flat stomach. "It might be in the safest place. I don't like these guys, but Special Agent Burke at the FBI says they're the good guys. And he respects them." Dec sighed. "Right now, I'm more worried about telling Mel and her crew about Lars."

Ronin pulled Peri closer. Right now, he didn't care about traitorous scientists, abandoned ice cities, and dangerous artifacts.

On this mission, he'd found something far more amazing and far more important. And now, he had to work out how to love her and keep her happy.

"Let's just go home," Peri whispered against him.

"I'd like that." He pressed a kiss to the top of her head.

PERI'S FINGERS dug into the bedcovers in her room at Aurora Station as Ronin powered into her from behind.

"Deeper," he growled. His hands clamped her hips, tilting her. On the next thrust of his cock, he hit deep, and a long moan escaped her lips.

He was so big, thick, and hard inside her.

"So fucking good, Peri." His voice was low and thick. "I'm going to fuck you forever. Every day."

"Yes." She thrust back to meet him. Right now, they were warm, safe, and everything was right in her world. Right now, there was only her and Ronin.

He slammed deep and then covered her body with his, pressing against her back. His mouth found hers and she tilted her head to give him better access. The kiss was wild and rough.

They were alive, and this was the best celebration of that.

One of his hands slid under her, skating down her belly. When his fingers brushed her clit, she bit down on her lip to stifle her cries. His hips stopped, and he held himself deep inside her.

"Don't stop, Ronin!"

"I won't, baby." His fingers moved down, touching where his cock was lodged. "Just want to feel you stretched so nicely around me."

"Ronin, move."

"So impatient." He pulled back and then drove back into her.

Peri pressed her head against the bed. "Feels so good."

"Yes. Say my name, Peri."

"Ronin." She moaned helplessly as he kept pumping into her, pushing back to meet him. "My Ronin."

"I love hearing you say my name when I have my cock inside you. Touch your clit, Peri. I want to feel you come on my cock."

She followed his order, touching the swollen nub. She moaned again.

"So damn sexy." His voice was guttural. "Let me feel you come and then I'm going to fuck you really hard. So you know who you belong to."

Another flick of her finger and pleasure battered her in a fierce wave. She cried out his name, everything an assault on her senses—the thick girth of him stretching her, the wash of intense pleasure shaking through her body, the heat pumping off him, the harsh groans escaping him with each hard thrust.

Then he thrust deep and held himself there, his body shuddering. A groan tore from him and she felt his release pour inside her.

They collapsed on the bed, his weight pinning her down. She didn't care. She'd never felt this good and she never wanted to move.

"Love you, Peri." His lips pressed to the back of her neck. "Be mine."

Warmth burst in her chest. "I already am."

"When we get back to Denver...I don't want to be apart from you."

She heard the faint hesitation buried in his voice. She

nudged him and had just enough energy to turn to face him.

"My house is big enough for one sexy former G-Man." She cupped his face. "We've been through a lot in a short period of time—" she felt him tense "—but we both know we have the real deal here. I'm not letting you get away, Ronin." She snuggled into him. "You're mine now."

He relaxed against her. "I think I've been waiting for you my entire life."

---

DARCY WARD RACED to finish up for the day. She started shutting down her computer system and then glanced at her watch. She needed to be at Peri and Ronin's house in time for the barbecue. She was bringing Ronin's secret gift for Peri.

Who knew the big, bad, and lethal Coop had a romantic streak?

The entire THS team was gathering at Peri and Ronin's to celebrate the successful Antarctic mission, and the fact that they'd rescued Peri's sister and helped take down another Silk Road top dog. Oh, and helped save the world.

In the two weeks since the team had returned, everyone's scratches and bruises had healed, and in the biggest surprise move of all, Ronin Cooper had fallen in love.

Darcy smiled, shook her head, and tapped some keys on her keyboard. Coop had a surprise planned for Peri today, and Darcy couldn't wait to see the woman's face.

She was so thrilled to see Coop opening up and completely in love. She paused for a second, staring off into space.

Her brothers had fallen in love, and with fantastic women Darcy was thrilled to have in the family. Jeez, even Logan had taken the plunge. Why couldn't Darcy find the right guy?

Her heels clicked on the concrete floor as she headed over to turn the light in the kitchenette off. She pushed all the silly notions about finding romance away, and in her head, she ran through her plan, instead. She needed to get home and change, then load her car up with all the food and drinks she had for the barbecue, plus the big surprise. She'd put herself in charge of the catering. If that task was assigned to her brothers, they'd end up eating chips and hot dogs. Darcy suppressed a shudder.

"Darcy?"

The too-familiar male voice startled her. Her head jerked up, and she saw a rugged face filling one of her screens. A screen she'd just turned off.

"Burke." How the hell had Agent Arrogant and Annoying broken into her system? Again. "How did you crack my system?" Annoyance raced through her as she strode across the space. "You might be the FBI, but this time I'm going to have you arrested—"

His intense, unsmiling face stared at her, his green eyes glittering, even across the screen. "I need you."

Darcy's heart skipped a beat. "What?"

"I need you for a mission," he said.

*Oh.* A mission. Right. "You want to hire THS?"

The FBI agent nodded. "But this job will require *your* special skills. On site."

What? Darcy dropped down into her chair. She didn't go into the field. "No."

"You owe me, remember. I believe a certain team saved your brother in Antarctica."

She sucked in a deep breath. "Tell me."

"There's an exhibit coming up at the Dashwood Museum."

Darcy tilted her head. She knew that after the Smithsonian, the Dashwood was one of the most respected museums in Washington DC. "Go on."

"A private collection of previously unseen artifacts is going on display. It includes one particular and very special artifact."

"Let me guess?" she said. "Something Silk Road wants."

Burke nodded. "Yes. Something I believe Silk Road's Collector won't be able to resist."

*The Collector.* Since Dec and the others had returned from Antarctica, she'd been running searches on the Collector, trying to find out who the now-sole leader of Silk Road was.

She crossed her legs. "Can't you flash your badge at the museum, and be arrogant and annoying—?"

"They believe their security is good enough, and they haven't broken any laws." His tone suggested he wouldn't mind throwing a few Dashwood employees behind bars. "I've convinced them to bring in added security...paid for by the FBI, of course."

"Of course." So THS would go in and provide security for this exhibit. It was something they'd done plenty of times before, although she knew the guys didn't love standing around museums all day.

She'd had the unfortunate luck to have dealt with this special agent far longer than she would have liked— Burke always rubbed her the wrong way. That also meant she could read that poker face of his pretty well by now.

"But it's more than that," she said, venturing a guess.

"I want you to help me set a trap." His face hardened. "I want you to help me catch the final leader of Silk Road."

She straightened, electricity spiking through her. "You're sure the Collector will want this particular artifact."

"Yes."

It was an opportunity she knew her brothers wouldn't want to miss. It was one she didn't want to miss, even if it meant she had to work side by side with Alastair Burke. "Okay. I need to talk to Dec and Cal first, but they'll say yes. I'll help you."

"Good." Fierce satisfaction crossed his face. "How soon can you get to DC?"

RONIN LED a blindfolded Peri up the garden path, ensuring she didn't trip or stumble.

"What's going on?" she said with a laugh.

"Just a few more seconds." He maneuvered her over a crooked paver, and made a mental note to fix it when he got a chance. "Ready?"

"Yes! I've been dying to see this present of yours since you blindfolded me."

He pulled the fabric off her eyes.

In front of them, all his friends cheered.

"Hi, Peri," Dec called out.

"There better be beer at the end of this," Logan grumbled. "Hey, Peri."

She gasped and grabbed Ronin's arm, squeezing it tightly. She stood there, her eyes as wide as saucers, in the middle of the front lawn of her little house, staring at the entire THS team. They were all hard at work. Dec, Cal, Layne, and Morgan were painting. Logan, Hale, and Zach were swinging hammers and fixing the porch, while Sydney handed them nails and wood planks.

"Ronin—" Peri's voice was thick.

"You wanted a home, and we're making one right here. I've never had a home before, just a place to sleep and store my things. But I want one, now." He cupped her cheeks, and his heart clenched at the sight of the tears glistening in her eyes. But he'd been around her enough to know they were tears of happiness. "I want to build a home with you. I love you, Peri."

"I love you, too, G-Man." She went up on her toes and kissed him.

The taste of her hit his system, always thrilling, and he bent her backward, deepening the kiss.

"Hey, give that girl some air," Morgan said from nearby.

The women surrounded them. Morgan hitched up her toolbelt, and Layne had a streak of paint down her cheek. Dani had her camera out and was taking candid photos, and Elin was smiling at them.

"Where's Darcy?" Peri asked.

"Here!" Looking as polished as always, not a hair out of place, Darcy came through the dilapidated gate. She smiled. "Sorry, I don't do manual labor." She waved a hand at a table set up under a nearby tree. "I have a carload of refreshments that need to be set up over there."

Logan pushed past. "I'll get them."

Sydney appeared with a bottle of white wine and glasses. "I think it's time for us ladies to take a seat and supervise."

Dani snorted. "You mean watch hot guys work and get sweaty."

"Do you think they'll take their shirts off?" a hopeful voice said.

Peri spun and Ronin watched her hug her sister. Amber's bruises weren't quite healed, but they were now a fading, sickly yellow. She was also smiling more, so he figured she was on the mend. The Butler women were clearly made of hardy stock.

"I'm hoping the shirts come off." This came from Elin. The FBI agent held out more wine glasses so Sydney could pour. The woman's gaze drifted over to Hale. "My man has an amazing body."

Peri smiled. "My guy isn't too shabby, either."

He mock-growled, and pulled her into his arms.

"Thank you," she said.

"I know you were taking your time to renovate, but I wanted to do something nice for you."

Her fingers stroked his cheek. "You know, you may

not have had a home before, Ronin—" her gaze drifted over to where his friends were working "— but you have a family."

Yeah, she was right. He glanced at his friends. He knew his life would have been a much darker, colder place without them. Hell, he might not have made it without them. He pulled Peri to his chest. And now, his life was filled with light and laughter.

"And you're my family, too, now," he said. "My home is wherever you are, Peri."

As Elin shoved drinks at them, Ronin watched Darcy wander over to talk with Dec. He saw Dec frown, his face turning serious. Ronin's instincts pinged and he wondered what was going on. No doubt he'd hear about it soon.

"Hey, what about this, over here?" Peri pointed at a stack of wood nearby.

Ronin shifted. "That's for the fence."

"Fence?"

"Yeah, the white picket fence I'm going to build."

Peri's smile turned blinding. "That sounds great."

"I...ah, have something else for you."

Her smile widened. "You're going to have a hard time topping this when my birthday comes around."

*Shit.* Ronin froze. He had to get her better things for her birthday?

"Here you go," Logan called out.

They both turned to see Logan with his arms full of a wiggling bundle.

Peri's mouth dropped open. "What the—?"

Ronin cleared his throat and took the dog from his friend. "This is for you." He shoved the beagle at Peri.

She closed her arms around the animal, pulling him close. "He's gorgeous." Her gaze locked with Ronin's, filled with love.

"He's a rescue, but only a year old and in dire need of training." He watched the beagle lick Peri's face in fits of joy. "His name is Porthos."

"Thank you."

"There's one thing you need to know, though."

"Oh?"

"He's half mine. He's *our* dog."

Peri set the animal down and he bounded away toward the food table. She grabbed Ronin's shirt and pulled him closer. "Come here, G-Man. I need you to kiss me."

So Ronin kissed her—the only woman he'd ever loved and would love—standing in front of the house that would be their home, surrounded by the people who were his family, and their dog.

---

I hope you enjoyed Ronin and Peri's story!

Treasure Hunter Security will continue in 2018 with 1) *Unidentified* (a novella duo) – which includes the story of former Navy SEAL and *Sea Nymph* captain, Diego Torres, and the story of how Professor Ward first met his treasure hunter wife, Persephone, and 2) *Undetected* starring Darcy Ward and a certain FBI agent.

For more action-packed romance, read on for a preview of the first chapter of *Among Galactic Ruins,* the first book in my award-winning Phoenix Adventures series. This is action, adventure, romance, and treasure hunting in space!

**Don't miss out!** For updates about new releases, action romance info, free books, and other fun stuff, sign up for my VIP mailing list and get your *free box set* containing three action-packed romances.

Visit here to get started: www.annahackettbooks.com

# PREVIEW: AMONG GALACTIC RUINS

## MORE ACTION ROMANCE?

**ACTION
ADVENTURE
TREASURE HUNTS
SEXY SCI-FI ROMANCE**

When astro-archeologist and museum curator Dr. Lexa Carter discovers a secret map to a lost old Earth treasure—a priceless Fabergé egg—she's excited at the prospect of a treasure hunt to the dangerous desert planet of Zerzura. What she's not so happy about is being saddled with a bodyguard—the museum's mysterious new head of security, Damon Malik.

After many dangerous years as a galactic spy, Damon

*Malik just wanted a quiet job where no one tried to kill him. Instead of easy work in a museum full of artifacts, he finds himself on a backwater planet babysitting the most infuriating woman he's ever met.*

*She thinks he's arrogant. He thinks she's a trouble-magnet. But among the desert sands and ruins, adventure led by a young, brash treasure hunter named Dathan Phoenix, takes a deadly turn. As it becomes clear that someone doesn't want them to find the treasure, Lexa and Damon will have to trust each other just to survive.*

As the descending starship hit turbulence, Dr. Alexa Carter gasped, her stomach jumping.

But she didn't feel sick, she felt *exhilarated.*

She stared out the window at the sand dunes of the planet below. Zerzura. The legendary planet packed with danger, mystery and history.

She was *finally* here. All she could see was sand dune, after yellow sand dune, all the way off into the distance. The dual suns hung in the sky, big and full—one gold and one red—baking the ground below.

But there was more to Zerzura than that. She knew, from all her extensive history training as an astro-archeologist, that the planet was covered in ruins—some old and others beyond ancient. She knew every single one of the myths and legends.

She glanced down at her lap and clutched the Sync communicator she was holding. Right here she had her ticket to finding an ancient Terran treasure.

Lexa thumbed the screen. She'd found the slim,

ancient vase in the museum archives and initially thought nothing of the lovely etchings of priestesses on the side of it.

Until she'd finished translating the obscure text.

She'd been gobsmacked when she realized the text gave her clues that not only formed a map, but also described what the treasure was at the end. A famed Fabergé egg.

Excitement zapped like electricity through her veins. After a career spent mostly in the Galactic Institute of Historical Preservation and on a few boring digs in the central systems, she was now the curator of the Darend Museum on Zeta Volantis—a private and well-funded museum that was mostly just a place for her wealthy patron, Marius Darend, to house his extensive, private collection of invaluable artifacts from around the galaxy.

But like most in the galaxy, he had a special obsession with old Earth artifacts. When she'd gone to him with the map and proposal to go on a treasure hunt to Zerzura to recover it, he'd been more than happy to fund it.

So here she was, Dr. Alexa Carter, on a treasure hunt.

Her father, of course, had almost had a coronary when she'd told her parents she'd be gone for several weeks. That familiar hard feeling invaded her belly. Baron Carter did not like his only daughter working, let alone being an astro-archeologist, and he *really* didn't like her going to a planet like Zerzura. He'd ranted about wild chases and wastes of time, and predicted her failure.

She straightened in her seat. She'd been ignoring her

father's disapproval for years. When she had the egg in her hands, then he'd have to swallow his words.

Someone leaned over her, a broad shoulder brushing hers. "Strap in, Princess, we're about to land."

Lexa's excitement deflated a little. There was just one fly in her med gel.

Unfortunately, Marius had insisted she bring along the museum's new head of security. She didn't know much about Damon Malik, but she knew she didn't like him. The rumor among the museum staff was that he had a super-secret military background.

She looked at him now, all long, and lean and dark. He had hair as black as her own, but skin far darker. She couldn't see him in the military. His manner was too... well, she wasn't sure what, exactly, but he certainly didn't seem the type to happily take orders.

No, he preferred to be the one giving them.

He shot her a small smile, but it didn't reach his dark eyes. Those midnight-blue eyes were always...intense. Piercing. Like he was assessing everything, calculating. She found it unsettling.

"I'm already strapped in, Mr. Malik." She tugged on her harness and raised a brow.

"Just checking. I'm here to make sure you don't get hurt on this little escapade."

"Escapade?" She bit her tongue and counted to ten. "We have a map leading to the location of a very valuable artifact. That's hardly an escapade."

"Whatever helps you sleep at night, Princess." He shot a glance at the window and the unforgiving desert below. "This is a foolish risk for some silly egg."

She huffed out a breath. Infuriating man. "Why get a job at a museum if you think artifacts are silly?"

He leaned back in his seat. "Because I needed a change. One where no one tried to kill me."

Kill him? She narrowed her eyes and wondered again just what the hell he'd done before he'd arrived at the Darend.

A chime sounded and the pilot's voice filtered into the plush cabin of Marius' starship. "Landing at Kharga spaceport in three minutes. Hang on, ladies and gentlemen."

Excitement filled Lexa's belly. Ignoring the man beside her, she looked out the window again.

The town of Kharga was visible now. They flew directly over it, and she marveled at the primitive look and the rough architecture. The buildings were made of stone—some simple squares, others with domed roofs, and some a haphazard sprawl of both. In the dirt-lined streets, ragged beasts were led by robed locals, and battered desert speeders flew in every direction, hovering off the ground.

It wasn't advanced and yes, it was rough and danger-ous. So very different to the marble-lined floors and grandeur of the Darend Museum or the Institute's huge, imposing museums and research centers. And it was the complete opposite of the luxury she'd grown up with in the central systems.

She barely resisted bouncing in her seat like a child. She couldn't *wait* to get down there. She wasn't stupid, she knew there were risks, but could hold her own and she knew when to ask for help.

The ship touched down, a cloud of dust puffing past the window. Lexa ripped her harness off, trying—and failing—to contain her excitement.

"Wait." Damon grabbed her arm and pulled her back from the opening door. "I'll go first."

As he moved forward, she pulled a face at his broad back. *Arrogant know-it-all.*

The door opened with a quiet hiss. She watched him stop at the top of the three steps that had extended from the starship. He scanned the spaceport...well, spaceport was a generous word for it. Lexa wasn't sure the sandy ground, beaten-up starships lined up beside them, and the battered buildings covered with black streaks—were those laser scorch marks?—warranted the term spaceport, but it was what it was.

Damon checked the laser pistols holstered at his lean hips then nodded. "All right." He headed down the steps.

Lexa tugged on the white shirt tucked into her fitted khaki pants. Mr. Dark and Brooding might be dressed in all black, but she'd finally pulled her rarely used expedition clothes out of her closet for the trip. She couldn't wait to get them dirty. She tucked her Sync into her small backpack, swung the bag over her shoulder and headed down the stairs.

"Our contact is supposed to meet us here." She looked around but didn't see anyone paying them much attention. A rough-looking freighter crew lounged near a starfreighter that didn't even look like it could make it off the ground. A couple of robed humanoids argued with three smaller-statured reptilians. "He's a local treasure hunter called Brocken Phoenix."

Damon grunted. "Looks like he's late. I suggest we head to the central market and ask around."

"Okay." She was eager to see more of Kharga and soak it all in.

"Stay close to me."

Did he have to use that autocratic tone all the time? She tossed him a salute.

Something moved through his dark eyes before he shook his head and started off down the dusty street.

As they neared the market, the crowds thickened. The noise increased as well. People had set up makeshift stalls, tables, and tents and were selling...well, just about everything.

There was a hawker calling out the features of his droids. Lexa raised a brow. The array available was interesting—from stocky maintenance droids to life-like syndroids made to look like humans. Other sellers were offering clothes, food, weapons, collectibles, even dragon bones.

Then she saw the cages.

She gasped. "Slavers."

Damon looked over and his face hardened. "Yeah."

The first cage held men. All tall and well-built. Laborers. The second held women. Anger shot through her. "It can't be legal."

"We're a long way from the central systems, Princess. You'll find lots of stuff here on Zerzura that isn't legal."

"We have to—"

He raised a lazy brow. "Do something? Unless you've got a whole bunch of e-creds I don't know about or an army in your back pocket, there isn't much we can do."

Her stomach turned over and she looked away. He might be right, but did he have to be so cold about it?

"Look." He pointed deeper into the market at a dusty, domed building with a glowing neon sign above the door. "That bar is where I hear the treasure hunters gather."

She wondered how he'd heard anything about the place when they'd only been dirtside a few minutes. But she followed him toward the bar, casting one last glance at the slaves.

As they neared the building, a body flew outward through the arched doorway. The man hit the dirt, groaning. He tried to stand before flopping face first back into the sand.

Even from where they stood, Lexa smelled the liquor fumes wafting off him. Nothing smooth and sweet like what was available back on Zeta Volantis. No, this smelled like homebrewed rotgut.

Damon stepped over the man with barely a glance. At the bar entrance, he paused. "I think you should stay out here. It'll be safer. I'll find out what I can about Phoenix and be right back."

She wanted to argue, but right then, two huge giants slammed out of the bar, wrestling each other. One was an enormous man, almost seven feet tall, with some aquatic heritage. He had pale-blue skin, large, wide-set eyes and tiny gills on the side of his neck. His opponent was human with a mass of dreadlocked brown hair, who stood almost as tall and broad.

The human slammed a giant fist into the aquatic's face, shouting in a language Lexa's lingual implant didn't recognize. That's when Lexa realized the dreadlocked man was actually a woman.

A security droid floated out of the bar. Its laser weapons swiveled to aim at the fighting pair. "You are no longer welcome at the Desert Dragon. Please vacate the premises."

Grumbling, the fighters pulled apart, then shuffled off down the street.

Lexa swallowed. "Fine. I'll stay out here."

"Stay close," Damon warned.

She tossed him another mock salute and when he scowled, she felt a savage sense of satisfaction. Then he turned and ducked inside.

She turned back to study the street. One building down, she saw a stall holder standing behind a table covered in what looked like small artifacts. Lexa's heart thumped. She had to take a look.

"All original. Found here on Zerzura." The older man spread his arms out over his wares. "Very, very old." His eyes glowed in his ageless face topped by salt-and-pepper hair. "Very valuable."

"May I?" Lexa indicated a small, weathered statue.

The man nodded. "But you break, you buy."

Lexa studied the small figurine. It was supposed to resemble a Terran fertility statue—a woman with generous hips and breasts. She tested the weight of it before she sniffed and set it down. "It's not a very good fake. I'd say you create a wire mesh frame, set it in a mold, then pour a synthetic plas in. You finish it off by spraying it with some sort of rock texture."

The man's mouth slid into a frown.

Lexa studied the other items. Jewelry, small boxes and inscribed stones. She fingered a necklace. It was by no means old but it was pretty.

Then she spotted it.

A small, red egg, covered in gold-metalwork and resting on a little stand.

She picked it up, cradling its slight weight. The craft-work was terrible but there was no doubt it was a replica of a Fabergé egg.

"What is this?" she asked the man.

He shrugged. "Lots of myths about the Orphic Priest-esses around here. They lived over a thousand years ago and the egg was their symbol."

Lexa stroked the egg.

The man's keen eyes narrowed in on her. "It's a pretty piece. Said to be made in the image of the priest-esses' most valuable treasure, the Goddess Egg. It was covered in Terran rubies and gold."

A basic history. Lexa knew from her research that the Goddess Egg had been brought to Zerzura by Terran colonists escaping the Terran war and had been made by a famed jeweler on Earth named Fabergé. Unfortunately, most of its history had been lost.

Someone bumped into Lexa from behind. She ignored it, shifting closer to the table.

Then a hard hand clamped down on her elbow and jerked her backward. The little red egg fell into the sand.

Lexa expected the cranky stall owner to squawk about the egg and demand payment. Instead, he scam-pered backward with wide eyes and turned away.

Lexa's accoster jerked her around.

"Hey," she exclaimed.

Then she looked up. Way up.

The man was part-reptilian, with iridescent scales covering his enormous frame. He stood somewhere over six and a half feet with a tough face that looked squashed.

"Let me go." She slapped at his hand. *Idiot*.

He was startled for a second and did release her. Then he scowled, which turned his face from frightening to terrifying. "Give me your e-creds." He grabbed her arm, large fingers biting into her flesh, and shook her. "I want everything transferred to my account."

Lexa raised a brow. "Or what?"

With his other hand, he withdrew a knife the length of her forearm. "Or I use this."

## The Phoenix Adventures

**Treasure Hunter Security**

Undiscovered

Uncharted

Unexplored

Unfathomed

Untraveled

Unmapped

**Galactic Gladiators**

Gladiator

Warrior

Hero

Protector

Champion

Barbarian

**Hell Squad**

Marcus

Cruz

Gabe

Reed

Roth

Noah

Shaw

Holmes

Niko

Finn

Theron

Hemi

## The Anomaly Series

Time Thief

Mind Raider

Soul Stealer

Salvation

Anomaly Series Box Set

## The Phoenix Adventures

Among Galactic Ruins

At Star's End

In the Devil's Nebula

On a Rogue Planet

Beneath a Trojan Moon

Beyond Galaxy's Edge

On a Cyborg Planet

Return to Dark Earth

On a Barbarian World

Lost in Barbarian Space

Through Uncharted Space

## Perma Series

Winter Fusion

A Galactic Holiday

## Warriors of the Wind

Tempest

Storm & Seduction

Fury & Darkness

## Standalone Titles

Savage Dragon

Hunter's Surrender

One Night with the Wolf

For more information visit AnnaHackettBooks.com

## ABOUT THE AUTHOR

I'm a USA Today bestselling author and I'm passionate about **_action romance_**. I love stories that combine the thrill of falling in love with the excitement of action, danger and adventure. I'm a sucker for that moment when the team is walking in slow motion, shoulder-to-shoulder heading off into battle. I write about people overcoming unbeatable odds and achieving seemingly impossible goals. I like to believe it's possible for all of us to do the same.

My books are mixture of action, adventure and sexy romance and they're recommended for anyone who enjoys fast-paced stories where the boy wins the girl at the end (or sometimes the girl wins the boy!)

For release dates, action romance info, free books, and other fun stuff, sign up for the latest news here:

Website: www.annahackettbooks.com

CPSIA information can be obtained
at www.ICGtesting.com
Printed in the USA
LVHW03s1530280618
582187LV00001B/59/P